Char is a level one chef, capable of imbuing magic into his cooking. Offered a job in a new city where he can further develop his skills and grow toward his goal of one day owning his own restaurant, Char undertakes a dangerous journey through the Spikehorn Mountain pass. However, deadly beasts, thieves, and dodgy recipe ingredients aren't the only challenges in the mountains. When the mercenary group he travels with is attacked and killed, Char wows their killers with his skills and chooses to join them instead of being left to travel on his own.

Figuring out how to cook over a campfire with only salted and dried ingredients is a unique challenge for Char, but the fighters promised to deliver Char safely to his new job once their own task in the mountains is complete. But the new fighters aren't everything they appear to be, especially Captain Fen, who makes Char think about something other than cooking for the first time in years. Surviving the mountain crossing was supposed to be tough, but surviving this new journey might prove impossible.

THE CHEF

PRINCES OF TOVAL, BOOK ONE

MELL EIGHT

A NineStar Press Publication
www.ninestarpress.com

The Chef

First Edition, August 2024

ISBN: 978-1-64890-794-4

Also available in eBook, ISBN: 978-1-64890-793-7

CONTENT WARNING:

This book contains depictions of graphic violence and kidnapping.

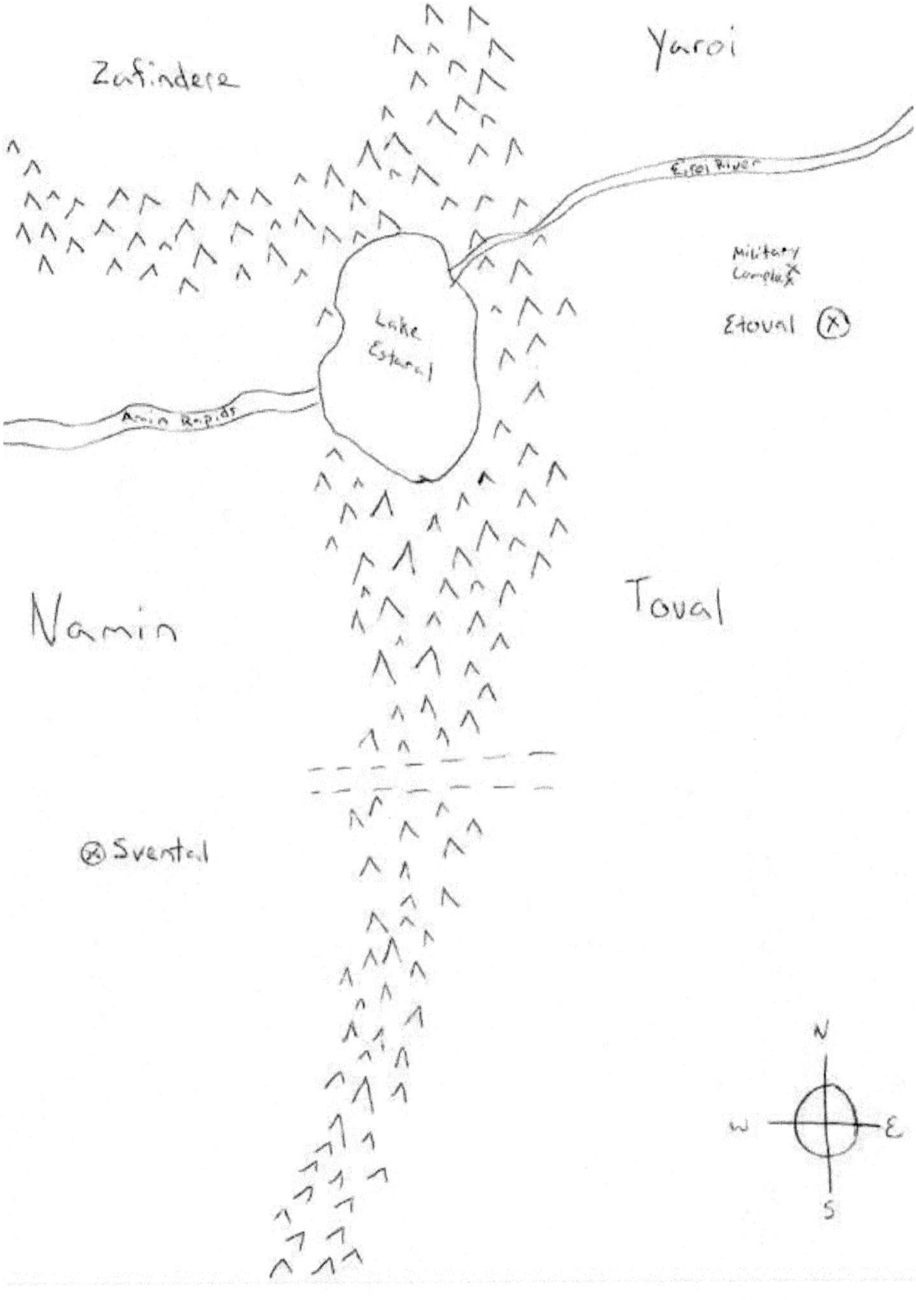

Zafindere
Yaroi
Eisel River
Military Complex X
Etoual (X)
Lake Estoual
Amin Rapids
Namin
Toual
(X) Svental
N
W E
S

Chapter One

THE SOUNDS OF battle had been going on for at least ten minutes. Char ignored them. The harsh metal clanging of sword against sword, the screech as a sword slid against armor, and the groaning and gasping of fighters as they exerted themselves—and ultimately died. Char let all that mess flow around him.

Keeping the oatmeal from burning was much more important after all.

Char gave the deep pot a stir, gauging the softness of the oats. Satisfied with the consistency, he opened the pouch of dried fruit and tipped it over the pot, letting half the pouch fall into the oatmeal below. The heat and residual water would soften and partially rehydrate the fruit, making it a perfect addition to breakfast. Char also put in about a tablespoon of brown sugar—calibrated to be enough for a pot this large without forgetting the natural sweetness the fruit would also add.

He glanced below the pot at the cooking fire that was mostly embers and decided it didn't need more wood. The oatmeal would be ready about the time the battle against whichever thieves had been airheaded enough to attack an armed mercenary company was over. After the mercenaries ate and tended their wounded, Char expected them to move out. He didn't need to maintain the fire to make lunch, since lunch would likely be jerky eaten in the saddle. At least Char had a pouch of his own homemade chicken jerky, carefully spiced with sage and smoked with onion and garlic. He didn't want to know what the rest of the band were actually eating when it didn't come out of a pot or pan of something he prepared; Char suspected it would be something gross.

The oatmeal was starting to bubble and blurp, very close to being ready. Char gave it another stir and then stopped to actually pay attention to his surroundings.

Sounds of battle came from all directions, so whatever enemy the mercenaries were fighting had tried to flank them. Still, the number of bangs, clangs, and groans of pain hidden from him by the thick brush and rocky terrain surrounding the campsite were diminishing, so the battle was definitely nearly ended. Char stood, went over to the bags adjacent to where their pack donkey was picketed, and pulled out bowls and spoons. He returned to the fire and started laying out his supplies until he had two lines of bowls, each with a spoon resting inside. The last bowl and spoon he kept for himself.

He was just reaching for the pot to fill his bowl so he could eat before the onslaught of hungry postbattle mercenaries when something hard tapped him on the shoulder.

Char glanced back and froze in place, the tip of a bloodied sword brushing against his cheek.

"No blood near the food, please," he said automatically.

But, as his eyes followed the length of the blade up to the owner, he wasn't met with one of the mercenaries he had been feeding for the last week. The stranger was tall and his fair hair, where it poked out beneath his helmet, was darkened with sweat. A splash of someone else's blood crossed his even features, and his hard hazel eyes glared down at Char.

"Er, hello?" Char forced out, unsure how to react.

"Captain, I think that's the last of them," someone else called from the edge of the clearing. "We can move out when you're done with him."

The stranger—the captain—only moved his eyes away as he replied, the sword not wavering against Char's neck. "Check their supplies. I want any orders or paperwork indicating what they were doing out here, and we might as well take anything of use." His gaze immediately returned to Char. "You're a noncombatant?" he asked.

"Hired to cook and maintain camp for the mercenary company," Char replied. "Do you want some oatmeal? It's just about ready, and it sounds like the people I made it for are no longer around to eat it."

"Are you bonded to a merc company or freelance?" the captain asked.

He was asking whether Char had any emotional investment linked to the mercenaries the captain and his people had just killed. Char didn't. What he wanted was their armed escort through the mountain pass and, incidentally, their coin. A lone traveler wouldn't survive the mountain lions, let alone the bandits looking for the easy pickings of travelers exhausted after the arduous climb. Adding a little spending money to help him get on his feet at his destination was an added benefit. Besides, aside from the mercenary captain, Char hadn't learned their names or really spoken with any of them. They hadn't been a friendly bunch, really more of a means to an end, so he wasn't particularly upset they were gone.

"Freelance," Char replied, trying to sound convincing. He would have shrugged, but that sword still hadn't moved. "I wanted to travel east; they wanted someone to maintain their camp. Getting paid is a side bonus. I'm headed for Etoval. No idea where they were going. We only contracted through to Marketon."

The captain continued to glare, his frown full of distrust.

"The oatmeal is going to burn," Char said. He really didn't want to die, but not ruining his poor breakfast was also important.

"Skinner!" the captain suddenly barked, making Char jump. "Stir the oatmeal and fill the chef's bowl."

"Sir!" someone called. A moment later the spoon scraping against the sides of the pot and the glop of ooey gooey, perfectly cooked oatmeal sounded. "Looks good," he added as Char's bowl was tugged out of his hands. A moment later, the bowl was pressed against his fingers for Char to take back, this time heavy and warm.

"Eat your oatmeal. Make sure we didn't burn it," the captain said, his voice low and silky with menace.

Char frowned at him, the first strains of ire building in his chest. "My food is *never* poisoned," he snapped. He didn't dare take his eyes off the captain, but he grabbed the spoon and scooped it through the bowl, bringing the contents to his mouth. Char chewed, swallowed, and opened his mouth to show it was empty again.

The captain finally stepped back, his eyes still on Char. He dug a cloth out of a pocket and started wiping down his sword. No doubt he was waiting for Char to keel over or to start foaming at the mouth. Instead, Char simply dug the spoon back into the bowl and stuffed more oatmeal into his mouth. He had worked hard that morning, getting the fire ready and prepping the food long before the sentries had dashed into camp to frantically report the attack and wake the mercenaries out of their bedrolls. He deserved breakfast, especially one that was well-balanced with fruit and grains, sweetened perfectly, and cooked to perfection so it slid across his tongue with an amazing texture.

The captain's mouth quirked upward on one side just the slightest bit. He finished cleaning his sword and slid it into the sheath at his hip.

"Looks like we can enjoy a hot breakfast today, boys and girls," the captain said.

"Yes!" Skinner cheered, diving for one of the sets of bowls and spoons. He was quickly echoed by about a dozen others, all of whom rushed forward.

Char stepped out of the way, glad to see someone enjoying the meal he had worked so hard on.

"What's your business in Etoval?" the captain asked. Someone gave him a bowl, and he started eating too. One eyebrow rose in surprise at his first taste, and he promptly stuffed a second spoonful into his mouth.

"My cousin invited me to come work in his kitchen," Char explained. "The letter is in my pack." He pointed over at the bags next to the donkey, which hadn't been searched yet. He didn't elaborate on why his cousin wanted him, although if the captain had been listening to what Char had already told him, he might have an inkling.

"Are all of those bags yours?" the captain asked.

Char shook his head. "Only the green one. The rest are dishes and rations, with the donkey to carry it all. I think the mercenaries had a long journey to go after Marketon, but I didn't ask."

A woman in hardened leather armor and chainmail pulled his bag out of the pile and yanked open the strings at the top. She pulled out his spare clothes first, shaking out each item and checking the pockets before setting it aside. Next she pulled out a rolled leather bundle. She undid the ties and unfurled it, revealing his knives, gleaming even in their sheaths, tucked into the pockets sewn into the case. She gripped one hilt and pulled it free.

"Look at this!" she exclaimed, thrusting the thin, curved blade forward and turning her wrist in a practiced movement.

"I promise that knife is much better for gutting fish than humans," Char called.

"It's really good steel," she added, looking at her captain as she spoke while tucking the knife away again.

"Why are the knives in your pack, rather than in use?" he asked Char, suspicion back in his voice.

"Those knives are for use in a proper kitchen with a proper cutting board and excellent conditions to clean them," Char replied, affronted that he was being accused of not doing his job properly. "A chef's job is dependent on the quality of his knives, and my knives are kept in perfect condition. A rough camp is no place for them."

She kept digging in his pack as Char continued to glare. The captain's lips quirked sideways again in a stifled smile of some kind.

"Ah-hah!" she exclaimed, pulling out his folio. She quickly brought it over for the captain to look through.

All of Char's personal documents were in there; everything he needed to be able to establish himself in a new city. His identification papers, his chef's license, personal correspondence—including the letter from his cousin—all filled the folio for the captain to read through.

"Charmaine Obenson," he stated aloud. "First rank, third circle, chef's college, Timmonsville University." He gave Char a flat look. "What the heck is a first rank chef doing cooking over a fire in the middle of the woods?"

Char sighed. He took a few seconds to scrape the sides of his bowl clean with his spoon, then chewed and swallowed the last of his oatmeal before responding, "As I told you. My cousin offered me a job in his kitchen in Etoval. The only way to travel over land from Svental to Etoval is through this pass, which the bandits know very well. As did the mercenaries, who didn't want to sacrifice a fighter to the kitchen for the week and a half trip through the pass. Our paths aligned. Besides, I'm still third circle. I have a long way to go before I'm qualified to run my own kitchen."

The soldier finished searching Char's pack without finding anything else interesting and moved on to the bags of food and supplies. She exclaimed a couple of times over the dried and smoked goods, far more than Char needed for this trip. The mercenaries had agreed to see Char through the pass and onto Marketon, but Char didn't think they had any interest in stopping to resupply there. Wherever their final destination, they had been in a hurry to get there.

Empty bowls were starting to stack up next to the fire. Char eyed them and the pot, which someone had helpfully moved off the fire to the ground. Everything needed to be cleaned, and the small stream that paralleled the path through the mountain wasn't too far away.

"Found some coded letters here, sir!" another solider called from where he was searching around the bedrolls.

The captain added his empty bowl and spoon to the pile and walked off, leaving Char alone. He was still under watch, since he was surrounded by the entire group, but with the captain gone a line of tension between his shoulder blades faded. They probably weren't going to kill him at this point, but Char didn't know what that meant for him long term. Rather than dwelling on it, he went over to the pot, which had been scraped clean of every morsel, and started putting the bowls and spoons inside so he could transport everything to the stream in one trip.

Char wandered through the camp, retrieving emptied bowls where they had been abandoned, and added them to the pot when he returned to the dying fire. He hefted the pot and started walking out of the clearing, but when he reached the donkey to retrieve soap and a scrubbing and drying cloth, the woman who had searched his bag stepped to his side.

"Where are you headed?" she asked.

"The stream," Char explained. "Only place to wash the dishes here."

She nodded. "Let's go."

Char retrieved all the washing supplies and then led the way through the woods in the direction of the soft burbling of the stream. The water was maybe a foot deep—two feet at the deepest part—and gentle. The raging, wild river he had encountered in the heights of the mountain pass had faded now that it had reached the lower slopes. Still, it was frigid. Char's hands and knuckles immediately started aching as he dunked the dishes to wet them down and got up a lather on his cleaning cloth.

Oatmeal was easy to make and—with the right additions—delicious. It was a bitch to clean afterward. Cold, dried oatmeal turned to glue, especially if it was given time to harden. He slopped a few inches of water into the bottom of the pot and left it to soak while he scrubbed and rinsed the bowls and spoons. Then he tackled the pot, which took multiple rounds of scrubbing and rinsing before rubbing his fingertips across the bottom produced a faint squeak to indicate it was clean. He shook out the pot to get rid of as much water as possible before drying everything thoroughly. Mold wasn't going to infiltrate into his dishes. Not on his watch.

They returned to camp and Char's guard went to speak with the captain. Char busied himself with repacking everything she had searched. All the food and dishes, his own bag, and everything from breakfast was tucked away again in no time. He hung the wet cloths on a convenient tree limb to dry.

When he looked up again, the captain was standing over him.

"Sir?" Char asked.

"Charmaine, I believe you when you say you don't have any loyalty to these mercs," he said. "What about to Svental or to the country of Namin?"

That was luckily a simple answer, although Char suspected the question itself was the opposite. "None. I was sent to a restaurant in Svental in the random lottery as part of the postgraduation placement program after Timmonsville. What's left of my family all live in Etoval or somewhere nearby within Toval."

The country of Toval—capital city Etoval—and the country of Namin—capital city Svental—were uneasy neighbors. Separated by the Spikehorn Range, the mountain range Char was currently traveling through, both countries coveted the lush farmland in the foothills on the other country's side of the border. Char had never studied politics or military policy or really understood all the machinations that went into keeping the peace. However, he had heard the difficulties inherent in moving large numbers of forces over the mountain helped. Certainly, even the small mercenary company hadn't had an easy time of it—especially since they were all dead.

The captain studied Char for a few long moments, his eyes hard and searching. He must have come to some sort of decision because he abruptly nodded to himself, and his expression softened.

"I have a proposition for you," he said. "Either we can leave you here with enough supplies for the three-day journey to Marketon, or you can join us. Our mission should last about two, maybe three weeks. After that, we will deliver you directly to your cousin's doorstep."

Char swallowed hard. He had been trying not to think about what his next steps might be until after the captain decided what to do with him. Now, his choices were equally difficult. He could attempt to finish climbing down the mountain alone, easy prey for the wild animals and the bandits. His chances of making it to Marketon at all were slim; his body would likely be left to rot where it fell, much like the mercenaries, and all of his worldly possessions stolen. The second option sounded better, but joining the captain was likely to be fraught with equal amounts of danger. Char didn't know anything about them, nor why they were in the mountains. Although, he hadn't really known much about the mercenaries either. They were a convenient way to be protected through the mountains—a means to an end. It sounded like he would get the same protection if he joined the captain. It would just take an extra two to three weeks to reach his destination.

"If I joined you, what would my duties be?" Char asked.

"Same as what you were doing for the mercs," the captain replied with an easy shrug. "Cook for us, help maintain the camp, and stay out of the way during a fight."

Joining sounded like a more certain way to survive. Char didn't really have a choice. He stuck out his hand to shake.

"Call me Char. Pleasure to be working with you, Captain."

Chapter Two

THEY TRAVELED FAST the rest of the first day. After loading the donkey and locating Char's pony, they led Char about a mile through the woods to their own camp, which they then cleaned and packed up. Then it was into the saddles, and they continued heading even farther away from the usual mountain path. They moved as quickly as the narrow path they were following allowed between the trees, rocks, and stream. They only stopped to rest the horses around lunch, during which Char enjoyed his homemade jerky.

About midafternoon, Captain Fendle abruptly turned their band north, following a game trail that wound through the trees and brush. The next few hours were slower going. They were forced to reduce their horses to a walk as they went single file down the winding trail. Char was beginning to wonder if they were going to stop at all, or whether they were going to travel through the night too, when they stepped out into a long clearing.

"Quick camp tonight," Captain Fendle called as he dismounted. "Fast, before we lose the last of the sun."

Captain Fendle was right. While they still had a good couple of hours before sunset, beneath the thick canopy of the trees the light was vanishing swiftly.

"What's a quick camp?" Char asked Roe as he dismounted with the group. The name Roe was no doubt short for something, but Char knew better than to ask what. She was the soldier who had searched his bags, and she had stayed close by throughout the day. Roe was likely assigned to watch him.

"Bedrolls and canvas for shelter, rather than putting up tents. Makes us more mobile and takes up less space," she explained. "I'm on tent duty, so I'll get your bedroll laid out and tie a bit of canvas overhead for you."

"Tent duty?" Char asked, wondering how they figured out assignments like that.

Roe nodded. "Better than latrine duty. Come find me later, and I'll show you where you're sleeping." She trotted off with a wave, heading to a man setting up a picket line. Char followed, passing over his pony and the donkey's reins and removing his pack, one of the bags with food, and a second bag with dishes.

"Where should I build a fire?" Char asked Captain Fendle, who was also handing over his gelding.

"There," he responded, pointing to the center of the long clearing. "Horses and latrine over here, bedrolls on the far side. The fire in the middle will give us enough light to keep an eye on both." He trotted off to oversee something else, so Char got to work.

He brushed clear a large space of old leaves and forest debris, all the way down to the damp earth below. The forest provided rocks to line a circle, and by the time that was done, Ralph had brought over cut logs and sticks. Char made a small pyramid and gently tucked some dry brush underneath. The flare of the match was bright in the dim clearing, and the brush caught immediately, jumping upward into the logs.

Char left the fire to do its thing, turning instead to his bags. "What's the water situation like?" he asked Ralph as he came over to drop another load of cut logs next to the fire.

"Tributary's over there," Ralph said, grunting and pointing off to the left with his chin. "'Bout a hundred feet? The track we're following was made mostly by deer going to find water. Captain will warn us if we need to start conserving because we're leaving the stream."

"Thanks," Char said, but Ralph was already leaving again.

If there was a chance they might have to ration water later in their trip, Char would make the dishes that required it now. Calculating for thirteen—twelve soldiers...mercenaries...whatever the fighters he was traveling with called themselves—plus himself, Char started pulling out dishes and ingredients.

"Hey, Captain told me to lend you a hand," Roe said as she jogged up to the fire. "What do you need?"

"Water, for right now. Enough to fill this pot to about here," he explained, pointing to a line about three inches below the lip of his four-gallon pot.

"On it!" Roe grabbed two smaller pots with handles to make it easy to hang them over a fire and dashed off.

Char checked the fire was going strong, wishing he could hurry the process of getting good coals. Roe took three trips to fill the pot, and then she joined Char, sitting down in the cleared space next to the fire to wait.

Horses were picketed, fed, and watered, latrines dug, bedrolls with canvas tied to tree limbs above all laid out, and the fighters were starting to join them around the fire by the time the fire had died down enough to start cooking.

Char placed the grill over the fire, setting the four legs firmly in the earth so it wouldn't tip, and then moved the pot of water on top to start heating. Camping food for long trips was dried, salted, dried and salted, or the rare food that didn't spoil quickly. His options were therefore limited, but between the fighters' own supplies and what they took from the dead mercenaries, Char had plenty of options within those categories.

He diced salt-cured beef into half-inch cubes and julienned dried mushrooms, setting both aside when he was done. By the time he located the pouch of dried peas, the water was boiling. He let it go for a full minute before ladling some into one of the pots Roe had abandoned, setting that onto the fire to continue boiling. Once the smaller pot was going strong, Char dumped in an entire bag of dried quadretti; the small pasta squares immediately starting to plump up. Next, he placed two large, deep-sided iron skillets onto the grill. He ladled about a quarter cup of the pasta-flavored water into each before dropping all three dried ingredients inside. Dried spices were next: rosemary, dill, garlic, onion, and a touch of red pepper. No additional salt, because the beef was already salty. The dried ingredients soaked up the water almost immediately, rehydrating and starting to steam. A sauce was next. He macerated sundried tomatoes, which then got their own pot, another complement of spices, and a full cup of the pasta water.

By the time he had the sauce set aside to simmer, the quadretti was done. Char used a slotted spoon to remove the pasta, halving it into two portions, which he split into the two skillets with the meat.

"That smells…" Roe sniffed, inhaling through her nose for a while, then grinned. "It's gonna be better than the oatmeal."

"I hope so," Char replied. "It would be tastier with fresh ingredients—tomatoes, garlic, porcinis, and bellas—but I think it will still be edible." Some red wine for the sauce would also help add complexity to the flavor profile, but Char was impressed by the variety of ingredients he did have to work with. He didn't have to forage, and he wasn't butchering freshly caught meat, so he wasn't going to complain.

He gripped the skillet handle and lifted it at an angle, jerking his wrist to make the ingredients flip and mix together. He switched to the second skillet and did the same.

"Isn't that hot?" Roe asked, reaching out to touch the handle of the first skillet. She yanked her hand away with a hiss before she touched the metal.

Char looked down at his bare hands and shrugged. "I'm a level one chef," he replied, which should have been enough explanation. At Roe's blank look, echoed by a number of the fighters around them, he continued. "To reach level one, you have to master the use of magic in cooking." A chef could be capable of making the most complex, sophisticated dishes, but if they couldn't master the use of their magic—something inherent in every living creature—the highest they could ever aspire was a level two. "I graduated as a level one, tier five chef and completed my apprenticeship, so I'm a tier three now. Working as an underchef for my cousin will help me pass the tests to achieve tier two, I hope. You have to be tier two of any level to open your own restaurant."

"I don't recommend eating at a restaurant run by a level five chef," Captain Fendle cut in. Level five demarcated an entry student and didn't even have tiers, but Char got the point he was making. "But eating at a restaurant run by a level two chef—which is the highest a very accomplished chef without magic can get—is an experience."

"And probably really damn expensive," Jeorgie added, making everyone laugh.

"If Char's a level one, doesn't that mean we're getting really, really spoiled right now?" Roe asked.

"That's exactly what it means," Fendle said. "Don't get used to it. I doubt our next assignment will include co-opting a chef in the middle of the woods." He clapped Roe on the shoulder before turning to Char. "How much longer?"

Char stirred the sauce, which had thickened enough he would call it palatable. Not really a proper tomato sauce, but it wasn't runny, watery soup, so it would have to do. Char poured it over the contents of both skillets, gave them another flip to mix, and then looked at the group.

"Who has the plates and forks?"

Near-absolute silence filled the clearing for the next ten minutes. Only the occasional scrape of a fork on plate, or the slurp of someone licking sauce off their lips could be heard, which only served to punctuate how little other noise there was. Plates had been brought out to the sentries, in addition to the fighters around the fire stuffing their own faces.

Char was pleased with the result. The peas had fully rehydrated, so they gave a pleasant pop when he bit down, the meat provided a nice chew, the salt gave his taste buds a needed bit of zing, and the sauce, while looser than he would have liked, complemented the overall flavors and provided a tart acidity to combat the otherwise plainness of the pasta. As he feared, the dish lacked for wine, and a variety of mushroom types would have elevated it from good to excellent, but Char cleared his plate as efficiently as the rest of the group, regardless. He still finished before the rest, since he didn't take the extra time to lick his plate clean.

Char left his dishes adjacent to the fire—starting the stack of dirty items to be cleaned—and dug through his bags again. He pulled out the large diffuser and a pouch of one of his specially made travel teas. Dried orange peel for extra vitamins, chamomile for sleep, rosehips to alleviate any saddle soreness, and hibiscus for more vitamins and a punch of flavor. He filled a smaller pot with the still-boiling water from the larger one. By the time he set the small pot down on the ground and hooked the diffuser in place, the water had cooled to the exact temperature for herbal tea.

"If you bring out the cups, we can have some tea before bed. The rest of the water in the big pot is sanitized if you have any canteens or water skins that don't have purification circles on them," he added. "I'll cover it overnight, so whatever we don't use now, I'll make breakfast with in the morning."

While the tea steeped, he moved the big pot off the fire and the grill onto an open patch of dirt to cool. Then, he tossed a couple more logs onto the fire now that the light from crackling flames was more important than the controlled heat of burning coals.

"Lemis, Yaroub, you're on KP tonight, right? You get dishwashing duties," Fendle said. "You can have your tea when you're done."

Ralph and Clarise didn't grumble, much, as they got up and collected dishes. Char certainly wasn't going to complain about not having to scrub skillets in the dark. Instead, he doled out tea into eagerly held cups and relaxed by the heat of the fire, enjoying the first twinkle of stars overhead and the growing chirps of crickets and frogs out in the dark.

*

THE NEXT THREE days passed in exactly the same way. After a quick breakfast at dawn, they spent the day riding, following game trails and a path only Captain Fendle appeared to know. Lunch was even faster than breakfast, just enough time to rest and water the horses, before it was back in the saddle until the sun started to set. They stopped whenever they found enough space to camp, at which point Char got to work.

Variety wasn't really an option when supplies were limited to what the donkey could carry. He used cubed potatoes, diced meat, spices, and specially formulated travel oil for one meal. Quadretti, oil, sundried tomatoes and jerky softened for a half hour in water and spices, then seared directly on the grill for another. Even though he was forced to use the same ingredients, Char changed the flavor profile with the spices. Using tarragon instead of rosemary, for example, rounded out the end result in a completely different way. He had plenty of time to meal plan during the day, with nothing else to think about during the long rides. For the third night, he planned to make a hash of parboiled, diced potatoes fried in oil with a handful of every dried vegetable they had rehydrated and tossed in. And some of the meat, of course—since he had a feeling some of the fighters might mutiny if he fed them a vegetarian dish—which he would probably have to mince so it melded in with the hash. He wasn't looking forward to mincing salt-dried meat with the less than stellar camping knives, but he would make it work.

They finally found a clearing on the third evening. Char dropped off his pony and the donkey at the picket line, grabbed his supplies, and went to the center of the clearing to start the fire. Ralph was on kitchen duty again—they rotated nightly—and was his usual gruff self as he dropped off a pile of wood. Roe had already taken the two smaller pots to the river, by now used to Char wanting the big pot filled with water, by the time Char got the fire going.

"If you can leave that for a moment, I would appreciate a word," Captain Fendle suddenly said.

Char glanced at the fire, which was burning merrily and would need time to burn down, then nodded.

"Sure. What's up?"

Char followed Fendle across the clearing to the edge of the trees where they had a bit of privacy.

"Tomorrow evening we're going to reach Lake Estaral. My second reminded me you would need to know why we're traveling through the woods fighting mercenary companies if you were going to be part of our mission, even inadvertently." He trailed off, his hazel eyes shrewd as he studied Char, the intelligence in the mind working behind them clear to see. "You're really not curious at all, are you? The only time I've ever seen you show any emotion is when someone says something negative about your cooking."

Char flinched, drawing back a step and ducking his head down. He ought to be used to this. Phrases like that from partners, friends, colleagues, and classmates littered his history. "Do you care about anything but cooking?" or "I don't even have to ask what's more important to you: me or cooking. Obviously, it's the damned food." Char tried. He really did. But cooking was his life and finding time to fit other people in around that was difficult. That left his partners and friends feeling slighted, and so he generally spent his time alone. Just because he often preferred his own company didn't mean the words didn't hurt.

Cooking brought him joy, so he focused on that and tried his best to let everything else flow over and around him. Apparently, that was about to bite him in the ass again.

"I'm sorry!" Fendle's eyes were soft with remorse. He reached for Char as if to pat him on the shoulder or even draw him into a hug, and yet he returned his hand to his side a moment later without making contact. "I didn't mean anything bad by that! I promise. Just…anyone else in your position would have been demanding an explanation by now, and you've been content to go along with us without complaint. You confuse me, to be honest."

Char tried to let the hurt go. The feelings were like a sore tooth; if you poked at it while it was healing, the pain flared up again. Fendle didn't know Char well enough to purposefully hit him on such a personal issue, so he couldn't have meant to be mean. He deserved an explanation too.

"I'm— I love cooking. More than anything else, I really love cooking. In the restaurant business, you very rarely get to actually see or hear people enjoy your food, so being with you all has actually been a nice change. Figuring out what I can cook with such limited ingredients and dishes over a fire has been such a unique challenge. Yes, I do wonder where we're going and why, but this opportunity trumps that. I'm having fun."

Fendle grinned, and suddenly his captain's veneer faded. He looked five years younger, softer, and more approachable.

"I put a sword to your neck, and your initial concern was that I not drip blood in your oatmeal. I'd say you really love your cooking. Nothing wrong with being passionate about something. My father had to force me to leave the training ring when I was a kid and practically had to tie me to my chair in the schoolroom until he finally found an instructor smart enough to couch the math and history from a military standpoint to keep me interested. My brother says I love my sword more than our mother, which isn't true, but I do see how my words earlier came out wrong."

"Forgiven and forgotten," Char replied, smiling back when he realized his words were true. The hurt had faded, dissipated by Fendle's understanding. "Before I sidetracked us, I believe you were about to assuage my, erm, absent curiosity?"

Fendle blinked and stopped staring at Char, as if remembering they had a reason to be huddled together at the edge of a clearing in the middle of the forest.

"Right. I'm trusting you with this. Betray me and leaving you helpless on the side of a mountain will be the least of your worries." His hard glare returned, and he stared Char down for a long moment before looking away. Magic flared, a gentle green light that meant it was military. Char's was blue for household-type magic. The back of Fendle's hand glowed for a brief second in the pattern of the House of Etoval. "We're a special mercenary group hired by the crown to investigate threats to the country and respond to them using clandestine means. We were sent to infiltrate a growing camp of mercenaries located near Lake Estaral, identify whether they are hired by or otherwise funded by Namin, and ascertain their final orders. We targeted the mercenary group that hired you because they were also traveling to the lake, and we're going to assume their identities tomorrow. I'm now

Captain Maximillian Greath, a known hedonist who would be willing to waste coin on dragging a professional chef into the middle of nowhere. I need you to be a level two—whichever tier you think is best—who can't use magic. Do you think you can help us out with this mission? I promise, when we return to Etoval you'll be well compensated."

"You don't look anything like Greath, you know," Char replied, although a growing excitement was building in his chest. He wasn't only working with fighters or mercenaries, he was working with spies! That put a whole new flavor to his cooking resume, even if he could never put it on paper or prove it. More seriously, he replied, "I'll have to dig out some hand protectors, if I'm going to pretend to be a level two."

Fendle grinned at him again, returning to looking younger and more approachable. Char swallowed, wondering why that smile made his stomach feel tight and fluttery. He usually felt this way when being handed a new or unusual ingredient. The excitement of the challenge coupled with the fear of not doing the ingredient proper justice with his cooking was what usually sent his body into overdrive. Never before had a smile come anywhere close, and Char didn't know what to make of it. He tried to ignore himself, focusing on more immediate needs.

"I'll do my best to play the role you need me to. Thank you for including me," he added. A glance over at the fire showed the coals were starting to glow cherry red as the flames reduced down to proper cooking levels.

"I'll do my best to continue including you in the future," Fendle replied. "Now, my stomach is growling, and I can feel the rest of the team staring at us, wondering when dinner is going to be ready." He laughed. "I won't hold you up any longer."

Char grinned back and returned to the fire. He got the grill set up, the large pot of water starting to heat, and pulled out his cutting board, knives, and ingredients, then got to work. He rushed a bit, since he could also feel the hungry stares focused on his back, so he wasn't pleased with the evenness of the cut he made on the meat and some of the potatoes were different sizes. Definitely not top-quality work, but he wasn't going to be graded on it so he didn't worry. Twenty-five minutes later, he started dishing out portions onto outheld plates.

The last plate was for him. Char plated his own dinner, his stomach also rumbling, and set the skillet aside to cool. He found a fork and dug in.

Smooth, yet firm potatoes mixed with the diced meat—still too salty, but it balanced out the otherwise bland parboiled potatoes—and the pleasant snap of rehydrated vegetables. Garlic, onion, a touch of red pepper to elevate the flavors. Except, as Char continued chewing, a strange, mild earthiness ran over his tongue. The flavor jangled, fighting with the rest of the ingredients. Subtle, with a slightly bitter aftertaste to his magic-trained taste buds, Char couldn't figure out what ingredient might have caused it.

"Did I put any powdered mushrooms in this dish?" Char asked aloud, mostly talking to himself as he licked the tines of his fork, trying to figure out how that peculiar flavor had gotten into his food.

"Everyone, freeze!" Fendle abruptly snapped, his eyes wide as he stared at Char with a dawning look of horror growing across his face.

"Poison," one of the fighters whispered, the word echoing through the silent clearing, and suddenly Char knew exactly what that awful flavor was.

Chapter Three

SOMEONE HAD MESSED with his food. *Someone* had *touched* his food!

Char growled. "Who put fool's mushroom in my hash?"

"Who was on kitchen duty today?"

"Ralph!"

"How bad is fool's mushroom?"

"What do we do?"

Char couldn't keep track of who was saying what or the growing panic, too furious to focus on individual voices.

"Ralph, did you poison us?"

"Absolutely not. I hate kitchen duty, but not that much!"

"Ralph's tried to poison us multiple times with his bad cooking, but not like this," someone joked, but it fell flat as no one laughed.

Except…someone *was* laughing. Char joined everyone in turning to look at Roe, who was grinning and giggling.

"Rosalyn Erch," Fendle snarled. "What did you do?"

"Not like it's worth hiding it," she replied, still laughing. "The amount of destroying angel you've already eaten? In six hours, you'll all be streaming out at both ends. If the severe dehydration doesn't kill you, in another six your liver and kidneys will shut down. There's no cure hidden behind a tree, not out here." Her smile grew as she looked around at them, particularly at the fighters who had started to cry. "My only regret is you realized it too soon, and I won't be around to watch you suffer." She ran her tongue along her molars on the right of her mouth, and a second later she clenched her jaw and something crunched. Roe looked directly at Fendle, her smile growing manic. "Randolph says hi."

Her knees collapsed as her eyes rolled back and a white foam filled her mouth. Her body flopped to the ground, convulsed once, and then went limp.

The clearing returned to silence for a long moment as everyone stared at her body. Then someone whispered, "What do we do?"

Fury. Absolute, boiling fury raged. "How dare you!" Char hissed at Roe's body. "How could you do that to my food? The spells for drying and powdering mushrooms cause bitterness. You need to combat that with honey! And powders absorb liquids differently! You ruined the texture and the taste! You destroyed my dinner!"

"Trust a level one chef to be more concerned about the taste than the fact that we're all poisoned," Jeorgi tried to joke, his voice stifled by the tears wetting his cheeks.

Char switched his glare to Jeorgi. "My food is *never* poisoned."

"You said it yourself," Cheryl argued. "There were mushrooms added to your food."

"Wait," Fendle cut in, holding out one hand to stop the fight before it could escalate. "Char, what do you mean by that? Do you mean no one has dared poison your food before, or that poison is rendered harmless?"

Char shrugged. "It's my passive magic field. If I stir it, cut it, heat it, or otherwise manipulate a dish, I negate the effects of poison. What I can't do is negate any flavor or texture changes," he added with a frustrated sigh. "I'm sorry dinner was ruined. It's my fault. I understand if you want to fire me and leave me behind."

He had gotten complacent, and he had been rushed, but that was no excuse for not tasting his food before serving it. His professors would fail him immediately. His cousin would rescind his job offer if he knew. Char was an utter failure as a chef.

"Whoa! Fire you? You saved us!" Fendle stated, his tone incredulous. "If you hadn't been here, we'd all be facing terrible deaths right now. Our mission would have failed, and Namin would have an unmitigated opportunity to attack Toval. You saved all of us, and countless lives in the future."

"I didn't taste my food before serving it," Char forced out, his voice barely a whisper. "If the Chef's Association found out, I'd be knocked down to level two, or even level three. I'm looking at years of retraining before anyone would consider hiring me in any capacity in any kitchen."

Fendle dropped his hands onto Char's shoulders and shook him gently. "You listen to me. You are in exceptional circumstances. They might have taught you how to cook over a fire, or how to make amazing tasting dishes using dried crap, but there is no way your school offered a class on rough cooking while on a spy mission to prevent a potential war. There is no precedence for it, and any review panel might fault you for not tasting your food, but they would never be able to find you guilty enough to demote you. I promise you."

"It's our fault anyway," Ralph added. "We grabbed the food from you before you had a chance to taste it. We're the ones who broke your protocol. Not you."

"See?" Fendle continued. He draped one arm over Char's shoulders and pulled Char into his side in a hug that somehow managed to send warmth through Char's entire body.

"So, we're not going to die?" Laurence asked.

Char looked up, finally noticing the rest of the group. Laurence was holding hands with his twin, Laura, and both had tear tracks drying on their cheeks. They weren't alone, Char realized as he glanced around. Most of the group had cried at some point, or still had pinched looks that said they were fighting not to. Char glanced up at Fendle, but his eyes were dry. His smile at Char was soft and full of relief.

"No," Char said, replying to Laurence and everyone else. "The fool's mushroom was neutralized. All you ate was some bad-tasting food, not poison. I promise."

"Right." Fendle released Char—leaving behind his warmth and comfort—and clapped his hands. "Char, do you think you could figure out how Roe snuck the poison into our food? And double-check the rest of our supplies to make sure it's all safe for us to eat without your having to cook it for us? Yaroub, Okenly, get a team together and search the body and Rosalyn's belongings. Then give her a traitor's burial. Somewhere far enough away we won't attract any wildlife to our camp."

The camp snapped into action. Char headed to the fire where he had left his ingredients and utensils for dinner. He was going to figure out how Roe had snuck poison into his food so no one would ruin his cooking again.

Licking raw potatoes wasn't how Char expected to spend his evening, but all he tasted was must. He took a pinch from each of the bags of spices next, but he didn't find any mushrooms. Char crunched his way through dried vegetables, dipped a finger in the various pots of water, and licked the cutting board where he had minced the meat. No mushrooms. Just a major shot of salt coating his poor tongue. Lastly, he licked the two cast iron pans he had used to combine the prepared ingredients and meld the flavors. He tasted the remnants of the spices—onion and garlic—some salt from the meat, and the starch from the potato, all of which combined into an acceptable, well-rounded palate, and then the sharp bitterness of magically dried and powdered mushroom killed it.

"She dumped it in the pans after I put in all the ingredients," Char said, his voice an angry growl. "Maybe when I went to gather plates? The powder didn't have time to fully meld with the flavors, so it wasn't in there long, I don't think."

"So it isn't likely she put any poison in the individual ingredients?" Fendle asked.

"I'll double-check anyway, just in case, but the potatoes and everything else I just tested were fine."

Char stood and looked around the clearing. Roe's body was gone, a small pile of things from her pockets next to where she had been. All the dishes were gone too—hopefully to be washed rather than dropped down a mountain crevasse—and Ralph came over and took the skillets away too when he saw Char was done with them.

Naomi was waiting by the pack donkey where the rest of the supplies had been pulled out of their bags and laid out on the ground. He joined her and settled in for a long evening of licking and tasting things he'd really rather not.

*

THEY CRESTED A rise around two in the afternoon, breaking out of the trees to see a massive lake spread below. Char could make out some trees on the far side, but he sincerely hoped they didn't have to swim or row over there since it was quite the distance away. Thankfully, as they started down the hill, the path curved, revealing a wide beach filled with about a hundred tents, many bunched together to show individual camps for the different mercenary groups.

About an hour ago, outside the range of any sentries, Char's group had stopped and added red and black patches with some sort of crouched catlike animal on it to their clothing. Some of the patches had suspicious reddish-brown stains on them, likely obtained when the previous wearer had been killed. Only Char, as the chef and noncombatant, wasn't wearing a patch.

"So you're Greath?" someone called as they drew close to the camp. "We heard the Blood Lions were coming, but no one said when you'd be here."

The man who stepped forward had a massive scar carved through his face, his left eye a milky-white ruin, but he was massive and muscled like a bear. An equally massive mace hung from his hip. The patch on his shirt over his heart was sky blue, with a thick, jagged line around the edge that looked like teeth.

"You must be Tarken from the Cannibals?" Fendle replied, his tone jovial and unconcerned. "Sorry about the timing bit. Had to wait for the money to come in first. You know how it is. Where do you want us to set up camp?"

"You're the last mercenary group we're expecting, so you get the area at the far end of the beach. A little rocky. Hope that doesn't hurt your delicate sensibilities," Tarken said, snark clear in his voice. He glanced at Char and the very heavily laden pack donkey and sneered. Char hoped none of the mercenaries had met Greath before. Tarken clearly hadn't since Fendle didn't look much like the bearded man with prominent cheeks and a receding hairline he had replaced. However, Greath's reputation for hedonism had definitely preceded him. That was the only explanation Char could think of for that sneer.

"I'm sure we'll manage. Let's go," Fendle said as he called out to the group.

They rode through the pathway between the tents, heading toward the farthest point in the camp, eventually arriving at a rocky outcropping adjacent to the lake and the woods.

"Let's set up," Fendle called, dismounting and stepping aside to wait as the rest of the group got to work, Char included.

Used to Fendle's way of setting up camp, Char located a good spot for a cooking fire in the center of the space. Flat without much leaf debris, yet still dirt rather than rock so he could dig downward to make a pit if he wanted to roast anything. They were going to be here for a while, so it made sense to set up a proper outdoor cooking fire. To that end, Char commandeered one of the shovels usually used to dig a latrine and hollowed out a bowl in the dirt. He lined the edges with rocks to keep the fire from spitting out and to provide stability to the grill, which he placed over the pit. There was enough room underneath the grill to safely add more wood, and the grill was also high enough Char wouldn't have to wait nearly as long for the fire to die down before it was suitable for cooking.

Naomi was apparently on kitchen duty. While Char worked, she brought all the bags from the donkey over, and once that was finished, started bringing wood next. Char left the bags packed, since that was the best way to keep vermin out, but he arranged them so cooking utensils and ingredients were to the right and the plates and silverware were next to the extra wood to the left. He got the fire started and sat back on his heels to watch it catch and the logs start to crackle before letting out a breath.

Preparations were done; it was time to start cooking a late lunch. Something lighter, Char thought as he dug through his ingredients, to get them through the handful of hours until dinner. Naomi had also filled his usual pot of water. He cut meat into small cubes and left it to soak in about half an inch of water to soften and hopefully remove some of the salt. A double handful of every single type of dried vegetable and mushroom went in a separate pan with water to do the same. Next, he pulverized dried quadretti until he had a fine powder, added water, and mixed until a simple dough formed. If Char had eggs, he would have made a pie crust, but reconstituting flour-derived pasta without the addition of fresh eggs meant his best bet was to make another pasta. He rolled the dough out flat and thin, estimating for enough to make about a hundred tortellini.

Char left the dough to rest, instead turning to the vegetables. He pulled out the rehydrated peas, which were nice and plump. He smooshed them into a paste in a bowl, mixing in parsley, onion, and garlic powder, and just a touch of water and travel-safe oil. Oregano and basil would have provided the depth of flavor he usually looked for in tortellini, and heavy cream rather than water to smooth out the pea puree would have provided a silky texture and a richness to the palate, but he made do as he had been doing the entire trip. Once the peas were fully mixed, he drained and dried the rest of the vegetables and meat and tossed them into the bowl and mixed until everything was thoroughly coated with the puree. Lastly, he had to actually make the tortellini.

He dolloped small spoonfuls of the mixture in straight lines along the dough. Once he had all hundred ready, he cut along those lines, creating a hundred individual squares. Each square became a pouch around the puree, and Char twisted and pressed on the dough until he had a shape approximating a proper tortellini. It wasn't perfect, but he was learning to live with minor issues.

"When do you want to eat lunch?" he asked, looking up to find Naomi, Ralph, and Fendle standing next to the fire, watching him work.

"Whenever it's ready," Fendle replied.

"Right." Char focused on twisting dough, finishing the last dozen or so. He popped a finished one in his mouth, testing it properly. The dough was gummy, the puree cold and slimy, but the tastes were as perfect as he could get them. He couldn't detect anything that shouldn't be there, and the issues with the rest would resolve with cooking.

For ninety-nine tortellini, Char used the big pot, salting the water before gently dropping them in and monitoring the strength of the boil to ensure the temperature was as exact as he could make it and the water wasn't moving so vigorously it popped the dough open. The tortellini started to float almost immediately, but the dough needed at least another minute to cook through.

There wasn't a way to make a proper sauce, not without tomatoes or cheese or cream. Instead, Char dug out some clean pans and coated them in oil and some of the same spices as were inside the tortellini. He added a large spoonful of starchy pasta water and let it heat slowly. When the tortellini were done, he spooned them into the pans, flipped his wrist so the contents mixed, and started filling outheld plates.

The food vanished far too quickly, but the mix of protein, vegetables, and starch was filling so no one came back for seconds. Char wished he had crostini to offer as a side to offer a balance of texture, but they didn't have any yeast, flour, eggs, or already cooked fresh bread to toast.

As everyone brought their dirty plates back, Fendle pointedly cleared his throat.

"I have been invited to a meeting of all the merc leaders this afternoon," he explained, his voice low so it wouldn't carry past their group. "Finish setting up the camp, and you all know the rest of your roles here." He waited for everyone to nod and begin to disperse before he turned to Char. "Your role is solely to cook," he continued in an even softer voice. "As long as you remember that, it doesn't matter who approaches you or what they ask. Okay?"

"I understand. Is there anything more I should do that would help?"

Fendle shook his head. "No. We've set up your tent and the ones assigned kitchen duty will handle cleaning the dishes. You can spend your day however you like until it's time to start cooking dinner. If you idle away the rest of your time without concern, that will help the illusion that you were hired only to satisfy my vanity."

Char nodded and grinned. "I can do that." He paused, then tacked on the worries spinning through his head. "Be safe in that meeting."

Fendle blinked at him for a brief moment, then grinned. "No need to worry about me. Although I appreciate your concern." His eyes softened and he dropped a hand on Char's shoulder, squeezing gently.

He left and Char held in a sigh, not willing to vocalize the strange, shivery feeling the warmth of Fendle's hand incited.

He didn't want to dwell on it, so Char went to go figure out where his tent was located. He would focus on getting his personal items situated so he would be prepared for the next few days in camp, and maybe that would banish the memory of that far-too-inviting warmth from his mind.

Chapter Four

THE LAKE WAS serene and still, a deep blue reflecting the almost cloudless sky. The only ripples on the surface were from the occasional gentle wind gust and the splashes of the handful of people doing something in the shallows off to Char's left. He walked in the opposite direction, heading away from the encampment, enjoying the quiet punctuated by birdsong and the occasional rustle of something larger in the leaf litter below the trees. He didn't go too far, though, not willing to get completely out of sight of his group. Fendle was probably correct that if anyone found him suspicious, he could be questioned or simply made to disappear, so he made certain the fire from his kitchen area stayed perfectly visible. Still, the peace helped the next few hours pass quickly, and Char was glad for the respite from riding. He wasn't looking forward to dinner, though, since he only had the same set of basic, salty ingredients he had been cooking with for days. He wanted a butcher where any kind of fresh meat was available, a dairy for milk, cheese, and butter—he desperately wanted to cook with butter again—a bakery for yeasted bread and flour to make pasta, and a large farmers market with recently picked produce as far as the eye could see. He wasn't going to get any of that out here; only dried, salted meat of questionable origin, pasta he wouldn't want to serve to his enemy, and vegetables that were more crumble than substance. Char was tired of it, but he would make do. He only had to remind himself that once they survived this adventure, he had the endless resources of his cousin's kitchen to look forward to.

Except... Char gasped and dashed closer to the edge of the woods, kneeling down to feather his fingers through the long green strands growing there. Tipped with little white flowers, the stems looked at first glance like overgrown grass. He bent closer, sniffing, and grinned. Sharp and pungent onion flooded his nose.

Char glanced around and his grin grew. This entire stretch of bank between the trees and the water was filled with the long green strands. So much of it that Char could harvest some the entire time they were camped here and not hurt the ecosystem.

Still, he needed to be careful. Lily of the valley, which was poisonous, was easily mistaken for wild onion. Everyone had enough of poisons, he was certain, and lily of the valley had a very different flavor profile to onion. Char dug down into the soft dirt, scratching away the muck with his fingernails, and gently lifted out what he was happy to see was a small bulb. A sniff confirmed it smelled of onion.

A whole field of wild onion. A whole field!

Char giggled happily as he dug out a couple more bulbs—just enough to supplement dinner—and cut a handful of stems too. He walked back to the camp with his booty and headed to the water to wash it all. The stems would need to be soaked to remove all the dirt and any bugs, but the bulbs just needed a good rinse since he would remove the outer layer of skin before cooking.

"Hey, Char," Jeorgi called from farther down the beach. Char looked up and saw him jogging over, something wiggling held in his hands. "Can we eat this?" he asked when he was close enough, holding his prize out for Char to look at.

Jeorgi was holding a fish so fresh from the water it was still gasping for air. The skin was greenish brown with darker brown stripes and had the distinctive slightly elongated snout of a yellow perch.

"Yes!" Char replied with an excited grin. "That's a perch and we can absolutely eat it!" Between the fish and his onions, dinner had the potential to be amazing. "How did you catch it?"

Jeorgi shrugged self-consciously. "We had some string and the thorn bushes behind our tents have curved spikes. A long stick and a worm, and here's what we caught."

Char mentally calculated for the group based on the size of the fish, which was only about five inches long. He couldn't offer fried fillets—they would deplete the entire lake in one night if he did that—but mixed with some other ingredients and a handful of them could be stretched a long way.

"I can cook it tonight, and if you catch another six or seven everyone can have some," Char replied.

Jeorgi nodded enthusiastically. He handed the fish to Char, who carefully juggled it between his fistfuls of onions, then dashed off.

"Ralph! Martin! We catch a bunch more of those and dinner will be awesome!" he yelled as he ran back to the group down the beach. A frenzy of activity started as Char headed back to his makeshift kitchen to start preparations for dinner.

He set the onion stems aside to soak in a pan. The bulbs he left next to the packs of food. He pulled out a large cutting board and what passed for a filleting knife, wishing he dared take out his own knife, which was sharp enough to carve perfect sashimi, but he knew he couldn't subject his blades to these conditions. He slit the fish down the middle and removed the innards, setting them aside to properly dispose of later. He curved the knife under the gills and above the tail, then gently slid the knife along the spine to remove the fillet. He flipped the fish over to do the other side, creating two perfect fillets. Next was the hardest part, particularly with the knife he was using. Perch skin wasn't edible, the scales too rough. He carefully slid the knife between the skin and flesh of the fillet, gripped the loosened bit of skin in one hand, and slid the knife along until the skin came free.

The result wasn't perfect, a B at most if he had done this in class, but considering the knife, Char was fairly pleased. Perch didn't have pin bones, so he was done with the preparations. He added the skin to the pile of innards and put both cleaned fillets into a bowl, which he covered and set aside. He would cook the fish closer to dinnertime, since it wouldn't take long, but he needed to get the bones started now.

He put the largest pot on the fire, pleased to see it had been refilled with water at some point, and chopped the bones of the fish in half. He removed the gills and any veins before dropping both halves into the water. Jeorgi came running up as Char finished, two more fish in his hands, so

Char got to work filleting and adding the bones to his fish stock. While he waited for more fish, he got another cutting board and knife and cleaned three of the onion bulbs, slicing them into quarters before adding them to the stock. The water was starting to steam when Jeorgi brought over the eighth fish, so Char told them to stop. He had more than enough for dinner. He added the last fish body to the pot, and then dug out his spices. Dried parsley was the main spice, so he added it liberally. Salt and cracked black pepper were necessary too. He was a little less generous with the powdered garlic.

Luckily, fish stock was supposed to be light and derived most of the flavor from the bones, so this recipe was perfect for when he didn't have access to proper spices. Given the conditions, the stock would take longer than the usual twenty to thirty minutes to cook. Char estimated forty to forty-five minutes, but he would check and decide whether to strain it or let it cook longer then. After the stock was strained, he would start on the fillets. While he waited, he pulled out the bag of dried mushrooms and spent ten minutes picking out the white buttons. He put them in a pan of water to start rehydrating. The white button had a gentle, meaty flavor that would add to the dish without fighting with or attempting to overtake the simple flavors of the stock, and it would provide a chew that was a different texture to the fish fillets.

Preparations finally done, Char looked up at the rest of the camp, wondering where everyone had wandered off to. Someone had cleared away the fish innards, and the fishy cutting board and knife were gone. More wood had been stacked nearby too. Clarise was over by the tents, Jeorgi, Martin, and Ralph still by the water—although they weren't fishing—there was no sign of Naomi, Jensen, or anyone else. They could be napping—

hidden inside their tents—off exploring, or off on some mission for Fendle. They could also be on watch somewhere in the woods, since they were in enemy territory and it didn't hurt to be careful. Char didn't know the details of who did what and when for this group, only that there was a rotating cadre who helped him when he was cooking.

The sun was starting to set, coloring the tops of the trees with deep yellow and gradating orange to red light. The lake shone pink and red where it reflected the fading sunlight. Hopefully Fendle would be back before dark, but Char would make sure to save him dinner if he wasn't.

The sun continued to dip until the fire became the better light to cook by. Char let out a breath as the beauty faded away into darkness and refocused on his dinner preparations. He finished cleaning the onion stalks and gave them a quick chiffonade. He sliced the remaining onion bulbs as well. The mushrooms were presliced but had plumped nicely. He removed them from the water and set them aside to dry. He cut the fillets into cubes a little smaller than bite-size so they fit on a spoon neatly. By the time he was done, it was time to strain the stock.

Most of the bones had liquified, imparting their flavor into the stock. The larger ones remaining were easy to scoop out. He carefully drained the liquid into the two medium-sized pots—since he didn't have a second large one—using the strainer to catch any remaining bones and the remainders of the onions.

The medium pots went on the grill on the far side of the fire, where they would remain warm but wouldn't continue to cook. Char switched to the cast iron pans, lightly coating them with oil before tossing in the sliced onion bulbs. He let them sizzle, stirring carefully, until they started to caramelize, before adding in the fish.

"We need bowls and spoons tonight," Char said, and when he looked up at the resulting bustle he realized a crowd of familiar faces was watching him work.

Each bowl received a generous portion of the stock, a sprinkling of green onion stem, some plumped mushroom slices, and a scoop of the caramelized onion and fish.

Fendle strode into the camp as Char was passing out portions. He was frowning and looked tired and fed up, but when the next bowl was pressed into his hands his lips lifted into a smile. He looked around until he found Char, saluted him with his spoon, and immediately started eating.

Char hadn't realized how tight his shoulders had been with worry until after they abruptly relaxed at the sight of Fendle's smile. He had zero idea what that meant or why he was so happy to see Fendle abandon the spoon and put the bowl's lip directly to his mouth. Instead, Char focused on filling and passing out the last few bowls, taking his own portion once everyone else was served.

The fish was soft and flaky. The caramelized onion provided a sharp sweetness that complemented the onion flavoring the broth and the bite from fresh onion stem. The broth itself was fishy without being cloying. Char would have been happier with some bay leaf and a more even cooking surface, but he had made another palatable meal. A light, crunchy starch—croutons perhaps—would have perfected it, but Char was still pleased to note the food from every pot, pan, and cutting board was completely gone by the time the crew assigned to wash up started making grumbling noises and collecting dirty dishes.

Fendle smothered a yawn behind one hand as he handed over his empty bowl. The crowd was dispersing, but they would return again for some tea once Char had fresh water set to boil. The big pot needed to be scrubbed first, though, because fishy tea sounded awful. Soon enough only Char and Fendle remained around the cooking fire. A second fire with un-cut logs set up for sitting in a circle around it had been created near the tents, so most people had gravitated over there.

Char added more wood to his fire, getting it hotter to boil water, and looked at Fendle. Even in the flickering light, the circles under Fendle's eyes were pronounced.

"I wish I had a proper oven to bake with so I could make cookies to go with the tea." That was the only topic he could think of to draw Fendle into conversation. Char didn't know why he felt Fendle needed the distraction, or why Char was the best one to offer it, but Char still had to try.

Fendle snorted, grinning at him. Char's ploy worked as some of the tiredness fell away. "I'm sure they would love cookies, but I'm also pretty certain we don't have any chocolate with us. Maybe our medic has some in case someone needs a sugar kick, but it wouldn't be enough for proper cookies."

Char shrugged. "The bigger problem is we don't have flour or a flour substitute. Or eggs. I can make really good, non-chocolate cookies too."

"Oh, I'm sure of that," Fendle replied, his voice certain and entirely free of sarcasm, which was a nice change. Normally, people quickly tired of Char's obsession with cooking; sarcasm and disdain crept into voices, along with sneers and snide looks. Fendle had more than enough time to develop that tendency but hadn't. Perhaps that was why Char was feeling so insistent about supporting Fendle as best he could.

"How are we doing on supplies, by the way?" Fendle asked. "The meeting this afternoon was basically a bitch fest, unfortunately. It appears the six mercenary groups here were all paid to assemble in this location, after which they were promised more pay to jointly attack an unnamed target. Apparently, per Tarken, we're to sit on our asses and run through all our supplies while we wait for someone to deliver the second set of instructions. Since no one actually knows when those instructions will arrive, all they could do was complain about not being properly outfitted for a long campout."

Char nodded. "We're okay for now. We have your supplies combined with everything we scavenged." He didn't explain aloud about commandeering all the extra food from the mercenaries Fendle's group had killed, but his meaning was clear. "Plus, tonight the only ingredients I used from our stores were some mushrooms and spices. The fish and onion we were able to forage fresh. With the foraging included, I would estimate our stores will last for two weeks, but if we think this is going to take longer than that, I can start rationing the second week and stretch it another week or so."

Fendle sighed. "I really hope this won't take nearly as long as two more weeks. The message will have to arrive soon since all the mercenary groups are here, so this should be done in a few more days. Then it's about four days ride to the city, and we can always stop in a town to buy supplies on the way if needed."

"Then I won't worry about rationing any time soon," Char replied with an easy shrug. "I'll keep an eye on our stores though. Just in case."

Fendle smiled at him. "I really am glad we decided not to kill you." He clapped Char on the shoulder. The flickering firelight was kind enough to hide the way Char's cheeks warmed. He felt as if he had kept his face too close to an open oven door, the blasting heat giving him the equivalent of a sunburn. New recipes, the chance to try unique ingredients, or an opportunity to learn techniques from a master in his craft; those were all instances that had his stomach fluttering and excitement flashing through him. Never before had it been from a smile and a friendly touch. Char had no idea what any of it meant, but he forced his lips to curve into an answering smile before his face alerted Fendle to Char's confusion.

Friendly chatter moved closer as the dishwashing crew started walking back from the lake. Fendle took a step back, releasing his gentle grip on Char's shoulder.

"I need to double-check the duty roster for tomorrow," he explained.

Char frowned at him. "And get some sleep." The words slipped out before Char could stop them, but Fendle only laughed at the motherly admonition.

"Yes. I'll get some sleep too." He smiled at Char one last time before striding off toward the other fire.

The washing crew delivered a full pot of fresh water, so Char busied himself making tea, hoping his odd, albeit not unpleasant, swirling feelings would abate soon.

Chapter Five

CHAR REALLY WANTED to make oat cakes. He had the oats and sugar, and the recipe didn't call for eggs, but what he did need was baking soda. There wasn't any baking soda in the middle of the mountain, and he wasn't going to magically find some growing along the lake's edge—since baking soda didn't grow. Substitutes like baking powder, egg whites, club soda, or even bananas were also a no-go out here.

He could make oat cakes without any leavening, but they would end up hard and tacky. Even with all the concessions he'd made to quality due to the conditions, Char could not justify something he knew would turn out extremely subpar.

Char sighed, but started measuring out water, calculating cups for the entire group. Once the pot was full of cold water, Char added a dash of salt before moving the pot onto the grill. He measured out the ratio of cups of oats, gently pouring them into the water. Most recipes said to wait for the water to boil before adding the oats, but Char found letting them absorb the water while it heated made for a softer and creamier final dish. Of course, oatmeal was always better when made with milk, rather than water, but there weren't any cows wandering by the lake.

As the water began to steam and the oats puff, Char added sugar. Oatmeal by itself was bland. It needed sugar of some kind or it wasn't worth eating. Usually for regular white sugar, Char liked to add cinnamon for a bit of extra punch. He didn't have cinnamon though. The molasses in the brown sugar he was using instead was just as good, albeit in a very different flavor profile. Unfortunately, the pouch of dried fruit was starting to run low, so Char only put in half the amount he would have liked. He couldn't compensate by adding more sugar either, since there wasn't too much of that left as well. They might not need to ration the rest of their food just yet, but Char could definitely see the squeeze coming.

It was too late in the season to be able to scavenge any spring fruits, and way too early for the apples or any autumn offerings to be ripe. Perhaps they might find honey out here, but Char wasn't about to risk getting his group stung by bees to collect some. Breakfast might end up being jerky and dried mushrooms—or plain oatmeal without any seasonings to make it palatable, which was even worse—if he wasn't careful.

"What did the fruit ever do to you?" Fendle asked as he strode over. Char looked up and realized he had been frowning at the bag in his hands.

"Just trying to plan breakfast for the next few days. I'm tired of oatmeal, but it's all we have. Problem is the oatmeal might also be inedible if we run out of sweetener." He paused, but a glance around said they were still alone; the crowd of hungry fighters were still completing their morning duties. "Any word from Tarken today?"

Fendle shook his head. "No, but if the people we're waiting for don't arrive today, I suspect some of the mercenary groups will pick up camp tomorrow and cut their losses. I'm hoping our erstwhile hosts realize that and don't leave us waiting." He sighed. "Anyway, sounds like oatmeal again this morning. Any plans for the rest of our meals?"

That made Char's frown return in earnest. "The potatoes are starting to sprout, so it's going to be potatoes all day. I'm thinking a loaded baked potato for lunch, although since we don't have any sour cream or butter I'm not sure I can comfortably call it that. Dinner will have to be mashed potatoes, but without butter and milk they won't be particularly creamy. The oil will smooth it out and some spices will make it palatable, but it will still be dry."

"Can you make a sort of shepherd's pie with it?" Fendle asked, sounding genuinely curious.

Char snorted. "I need eggs, cream, *and* flour. Pie needs a proper dough for a crust and the filling ought to be a proper béchamel. Although...maybe I could come up with a quasi-deconstructed version..." He trailed off, lost in thought for a moment, but the weight of Fendle's gaze forced him to glance up.

Fendle was looking at Char with the slightest smile lifting his lips at the corners. The look wasn't condescending or pasted on, but Char had no idea what it meant.

"What?" he asked, unable to let the mystery go unanswered.

Fendle's smile grew. "Has anyone ever told you how cute you are when you get so lost talking about food?"

"I'm—what?" Char spluttered out, his cheeks heating even as his swirling thoughts about potatoes ground to a sudden halt.

"Absolutely adorable," Fendle said, filling in the empty spot left by Char's inability to get any more words out.

"No. That's not true. I'm—" Obsessive bordering on fanatical were the nicest terms Char had ever heard himself described with. He couldn't make himself finish the sentence; the sting in his chest and his throat from just thinking about it kept those hateful words inside.

"Everyone else is clearly brain-dead, if they don't see how incredibly cute you are when you're captivated by food." Fendle reached out, and for a moment Char wasn't sure whether to be excited or frightened of the idea that Fendle might pull him close. But, instead, Fendle picked up the spoon resting on a plate next to the fire and gave the neglected oatmeal a much-needed stir.

Char stifled any disappointment, refusing to allow such strange and unwarranted feelings to surface. Fendle would change his mind soon enough after all.

Ralph and Laura arrived before Char inadvertently let any of his swirling emotions or worries escape, both apparently on kitchen duty today as they each dropped a load of cut wood onto the pile. They were quickly followed by everyone else, and Char was glad to let assuaging rumbling stomachs distract him from the confusion that was Fendle.

Emptied bowls were just being stacked into a pile for washing when a commotion from farther up the beach had everyone turning to look. A group of about ten people on horses had ridden into the sprawling camp.

"Looks like we finally get to learn why we're here," someone muttered.

"Right," Fendle called. "I'm going to head over and see what's up. You all know what to do." He glanced around until he found Jensen, his second in command, who nodded. Then Fendle's eyes drifted over to Char. He smiled again, reigniting those butterflies Char had just banished, and then turned and strode off down the path.

Ralph and Laura gathered the dirty dishes and headed to the water. The rest of the group drifted off, although none of them went too far away. Char left them to it. His role was to cook, and he had potatoes to worry about.

He grabbed one potato per person, purposefully picking the ones with the green stems growing from multiple spots, as those needed to be eaten first. Char headed down to the water too, a few feet away from the splashing from the dishwashing, and used a small brush to scrub the skin of the potatoes clean. Gentle pressure from the pad of his thumb snapped off the stems, leaving behind only spots that would soften while cooking and be perfectly edible.

When he returned to the fire, Char dug out a protective mitt for his hands. Normally, he wouldn't need the mitt, but they might be under surveillance, and Fendle had asked him not to reveal his abilities. He stuffed each potato deep into the ashes, under the rosy coals, where they would slowly bake over the next few hours. Char would have liked to wrap the potatoes first to keep the skin edible, but he was happy to make do with what they had on hand—which was lots and lots of potatoes. Closer to lunch he would do something with oil, meat, and mushrooms to give the illusion of a loaded potato, but for now he sat next to the fire and relaxed in its warmth.

Laura and Ralph returned and put away the cleaned dishes before drifting off to hover around the campsite with everyone else. They all carried tension in their shoulders as if expecting someone to sneak up behind them as they went about regular camp activities. Resetting tent stakes, airing out bedrolls, grooming horses, and other mundane, easy tasks were completed all while they kept looking over their shoulders, down toward the embankment, where Fendle had disappeared into a large tent along with the new arrivals and other group leaders.

Char sighed and sat up. He ought to wander down to the onion patch. Sautéed onions and mushrooms would be a good topping for his potatoes for both lunch and dinner. And now that he was thinking about onions, it wouldn't be too difficult to knock together an onion soup for dinner. If he ground up some of the dried pasta and used oil, he could make an approximation of a roux. The soup wouldn't be as flavorful as he would have liked without wine or nutmeg, but he did have rosemary which wasn't traditional but was an acceptable substitute since it would punch up the flavor. Cutting all the onions would take almost as long as actually cooking, but it would provide a different texture and experience to dinner than just mashed potatoes.

Decided, Char stood and dusted off his pants, ready to go harvest lots of onions. A shout from the direction of the command tent echoed through the valley, the actual words muffled. A second shout was followed by people erupting from the tent, group leaders dashing in the direction of their camps.

"Gather up!" Jensen called, striding into the cleared central area of their camp. Everyone joined him except for Jeorgi and Clarise, who ran to the horses to start removing their hobbles. Char hung back, staying by the fire, but he was close enough to join them in watching the path.

Fendle didn't appear. The other leaders all made it to their camps and their yelling galvanized their people to start moving, but there was no sign of Fendle having left the command tent. And Char suddenly knew what was about to happen wouldn't be good.

Chapter Six

CHAR SWALLOWED HARD, craning his neck to see whether Fendle might have gone to another camp momentarily, but a glance over at Jensen saw him frowning. Clarise started leading the horses over to their owners, and still Fendle didn't appear.

"Traitors! Liars!" Tarken yelled as he strode into view on the path. His fighters ranged behind him, quickly joined by the other groups.

"Mount up," Jensen called, even as Char moved farther back, almost to the second fire near the tents.

The sharp sliding sound of metal rang out as swords were unsheathed, but Char could practically feel the nerves of his group. There were only a dozen of them—less since two were on sentry duty and Fendle was missing—against all the other companies. This wasn't a fight they could win, but they didn't have a choice but to try, and Char would have to watch.

Jensen always had a horn hanging from his hip; Char hadn't

wondered why before now, but he brought it to his lips and blew three short blasts followed by a pause and three more.

The horn appeared to enrage Tarken since he roared. The mercenaries roared back and started to run, and the battle was on.

Char couldn't do anything to help. He was a chef, not a soldier. His skill with blades was exclusive to the kitchen. He didn't know the first thing about fighting, and if he tried, he knew he would only get in the way. Yet standing around and waiting wasn't really an option either. He might not be able to aid Jensen, Char decided firmly, but perhaps he could do something for Fendle.

He dashed into the woods where the trees and brush provided cover from the advancing fighters. The way was densely packed, Char fighting through tangling vines and spiked thorns. He tried to stay parallel to the lake so he didn't lose his direction. He also attempted to be quiet, but it was impossible when he was thrusting past branches and stepping on invisible sticks beneath the bed of crunchy leaves underfoot. Luckily, Jensen blew the horn again—three blasts followed by a break and then three more blasts—and that sound combined with the starting clangs of steel against steel as the two forces met helped conceal his noise.

The command tent where Fendle had gone was close to the entrance of the clearing around the lake. Char didn't know how much time had passed before he saw the tents of Tarken's camp through the trees. His heart was beating in his throat as he turned and crept closer. He carefully lowered a branch, peeking through the abundant leaves.

Four people were milling about in the middle of the camp. Three were wearing red-dyed and fitted leather and looked important. They carried swords at their hips, but Char was used to seeing his group of fighters every day; despite the swords, these three didn't stand like people who knew their way around a blade. The fourth was wearing the sky-blue and black patch of the Cannibals—Tarken's group—and appeared to be waiting on the other three. A glance at the tent revealed two more people, likely guards since both were wearing leather armor topped with metal vambrace and greaves, standing on either side of the entrance.

Char would not be getting in that way. However, he didn't see anyone else nearby. He slid out between the trees, crouching low and scuttling to the back of the tent. He fumbled his belt knife when he pulled it free, got a better grip, and thrust it into the canvas. Even though it was only an eating knife, Char kept all of his blades in peak slicing condition just in case. The heavy canvas split easily.

Another horn sounded: four blasts, a break, then another four blasts. And then a massive roar erupted, as if hundreds of people were answering the call of that horn. The forest was suddenly full of people a second later, all of them dashing into the camp. Char hurriedly dragged his knife down the rest of the way and slid through the gap, stepping into the darkened interior of the tent.

At first, he didn't see anyone inside and for a horrible moment Char worried Fendle had been moved elsewhere and all his efforts were a waste. Then he saw the body lying on the ground. His heart stopped and Char let out a sharp gasp, but his eyes were adjusting to the dim space, and he realized the body's chest was rising and falling. Both of the body's hands and feet were bound with rope. Char was still shaking as he crept closer, immediately recognizing Fendle's blond hair. His hazel eyes were open and furious, but they widened in surprise when he saw Char step into view.

"I really am glad I decided not to kill you," he whispered as Char carefully slid his knife into the ropes, sawing until Fendle's wrists were freed.

Before Char could reply "Me too," light flashed as the tent flaps opened. Char squeaked and accidentally dropped the knife.

"Looks like your lucky streak just ended," someone said as he stepped inside, his tone smarmy with just the wrong amount of slime. He cut off with a sharp swear, and Char looked up in time to see him draw his sword.

It was one of the red-leather guys, and he did not look pleased to see Char. He advanced and Char swallowed hard. Fendle was still tied up; Char was the only thing between him and the sharp edge of that weapon.

Except… Now that he thought about it, a sword was basically just an elongated knife. Right? Char was used to blades that ranged in shape from the smallest paring knife to the largest cleaver, which were nothing like a sword. But, if he could use his magic to prevent those from cutting him, perhaps the magic would work with a sword too? Perhaps, but that was Char's only hope so he had to try.

Magic was intangible. Every creature on earth had some inside them, but only through training and hard work could they access and use it. The classes at school were intensive, particularly for someone aspiring to be a level one chef. Char pulled the magic from the well inside himself with barely any effort, used to using it automatically and without thought whenever he was cooking.

The sword swung and Char ducked, tucking his head behind the protective shelter of his arms which he coated in magic and were glowing a faint shade of blue. The impact against his right arm sent him sprawling with a smacking sound and a flare of pain at the point of impact—but no feel of blood gushing or crack of bones breaking. Char scrambled back to his feet, galvanized as he faced the attacker again.

"Magic," the stranger said with a sneer at Char. "Etoval shows its weakness when it relies on such a crutch. Real warriors rely on proper training." He thrust forward, aiming for Char's stomach, but Char crossed his glowing arms and the tip slid aside, harmlessly bouncing off Char's forearm and passing to Char's left.

"Magic isn't a crutch because we use it to augment our prowess, rather than you Namin bastards who abandon all sense when you discover you can use magic instead," Fendle said, standing behind Char. He handed Char his dropped knife as he stepped in front. "Let me demonstrate."

He held his right hand out at shoulder height and widened his fingers to their full extent. As he relaxed them again, they started to glow gold, and Char swallowed a gasp.

Blue was classified as things of the home: cooking, cleaning, construction. Green was classified as things of the body: healing, psychology, and military. But gold... Char shook his head, awed. The royal families of the continent hoarded the secrets of their personal magic, which was far more powerful than most could ever dream to access. Char had heard not every prince or princess was capable of using it. He had also heard the training was far more rigorous than even Char's had been—and the training to achieve level one chef status had been incredibly rigorous.

Fendle curled his fingers as if he were gripping something and slowly moved his arm to the right. From empty air, he pulled a sword, the entire blade glowing gold.

"The saying the royals of Toval are always armed, even when naked in the bath, isn't a joke. Isn't that right, Prince Clament?" Fendle asked as he brought the sword up to a guard position. That was the only warning he gave. Fendle stepped forward and swung in one smooth movement. Clament belatedly parried, stumbling over his feet. At a glance, Fendle was clearly the better-trained swordsman. Fendle didn't stop moving, thrusting and slashing against Clament's awkward responses until Fendle twisted his wrist just right, and Clament's sword went flying across the tent. Fendle lowered his sword to point at Clament's chest.

"Surrender," Fendle instructed, his tone low and dangerous. "On your knees."

Clament dropped to the ground, his hands held in the air, and Fendle mirrored his movement with the point of his sword.

Before they could do anything else, the tent flaps flew open and Jensen rushed inside. "Captain!" he yelled, frantically glancing around the space, sword out and ready. He paused when he saw Fendle and Clament, and then lifted an eyebrow when he caught sight of Char. "Beaten on my rescue mission by our chef," he said, grinning. "We were wondering where you'd gotten to. Glad you're okay."

"I'm glad he beat you here too," Fendle replied with his own smile. "He definitely saved my life. Anyway, what's the status out there? I heard the horns go, but that's about it."

"Reinforcements arrived as requested, led by Captain Zain. She's madder than a wet hen about having to hide in the woods for two days while we enjoyed our cushy tents, so good luck with that, but she's rounding up the last of the surviving mercs. She has someone processing them per the mercenary code, so we'll slap some fines on them, give their group the black mark they deserve for attempting to attack us, and send them on their way. We thought we'd missed one of the Namin bastards, so Captain Zain will be happy to know you nabbed him for us. Might offset the madder than a wet hen issue. Might not." He shrugged.

"Casualties?" Fendle asked.

"Clarise is the worst, but the healers got to her quickly, so she should survive. I don't know if she'll swing a sword again, but her wife will be happy to have her back and retired with honors. Everyone else is like me. Bumps, bruises, and cuts, but nothing worse." Jensen indicated his arm that had a nasty slash through the sleeve and was bleeding sluggishly, but not dangerously. "Mercs just haven't got the training to compete with the royal guard, you know?"

Char stifled a cough of surprise, choking as he swallowed wrong. Fendle used gold magic. Jensen was a royal guard. That could only mean one thing.

"Thanks for the update," Fendle replied after glancing over at Char to make sure he was okay. "I'll see if I can do something to assuage Captain Zain's ire. Can you take our guest, Prince Clament, somewhere more comfortable?"

Jensen's grin took on a sharp edge. "I'd be happy to." He turned to Clament and pointed his sword at him. "Up. Let's go."

Clament sneered, but obeyed, walking out of the tent with Jensen right behind him, leaving Char alone with Fendle.

Spending time with Fendle was usually a pleasure and a confusion, but never before had Char felt this uncertain. Fendle was definitely one of the princes of Toval and Char had no business hanging out with him like they were friends.

"I know who you are too, you know," Fendle said suddenly. "Charmaine Obenson is your public name, same as Fendle is the one I use whenever I'm on a mission."

Char grimaced. Since his cousin worked in the palace in Etoval, it was no surprise a prince of Toval knew about their family.

"You're Charmaine Oba-Musen. If chefs could have golden magic, the Musen family would wield it. They're also the only ones with the ability to develop passive magic that neutralizes poison. In many ways, you're a more important person than I am. Any dish you make is worth its weight in gold and platinum."

"You know who I am," Char replied, exhausted by the day and suddenly feeling bold. "Who are you exactly?"

"Prince Fenwick, fourth child of King Aurelius and Queen Trina, but as fourth I'm barely in line for the throne, especially since two of my older siblings have already had kids. Mostly, I'm referred to as Commander Fenwick of the Royal Guard, but please, call me Fen." He sounded as exhausted as Char felt, but his smile was as gentle and welcoming as always. He walked to the tent flaps and pulled one side open, holding it back for Char. It was only as Char passed him that he realized Fendle's sword had vanished. No. *Fen's* sword had vanished. Prince Fen, Commander Fen—he had all these fancy titles, and yet all Char could focus on was the tilt of his lips as he smiled and the bright sparkle in his eye as he watched Char walk by.

Back out in the bright sunlight, Char was able to see Fen's face clearly. The left side was swollen and purpling, and his lip bloodied as if he had been backhanded at some point.

"You're hurt!" He reached out without thinking to trail his fingertips over the puffy cheek, then snatched them back when Fen sucked in a sudden breath. "Sorry!" Char stuffed his errant fingers in his pocket. "I didn't mean to make it worse."

"You didn't—" Fen began but stopped when a woman in full armor stomped into view. She had her helmet under one arm, revealing a gorgeous arrangement of thick braids keeping her black hair tight to her scalp. She was tall and powerful looking, her dark skin gleaming in the late morning sun, especially against the shine of her breastplate, which had the dragon and sickle emblem of Toval etched into it.

"Now that I'm done cleaning up your mess, that's when you show up?" she snapped, scowling at Fen.

"Hey, Z. Glad you made it." Fen's reply was nonchalant and his grin at her mischievous as if he wanted to induce her to deepen her scowl—which she did, growling at him. A man wearing brown breeches and a light green tunic with the healer's college insignia on the breast pocket walked up to Fen and, without asking, placed one hand over Fen's cheek. The hand glowed green and when the healer pulled away, the swelling had gone down significantly. Fen was still bruised, but at least the damage was fixed.

"Took us less than five minutes from the time your second blew the horn, even in these conditions. If my soldiers don't get a commendation, it'll be your head." Captain Zain—she had to be the captain Jensen had mentioned earlier—snorted. "Not a single couch potato among them."

"My potatoes!" Char gasped out, reminded of the lunch he had been in the midst of preparing. He dashed off, heading back to his cooking fire.

"Who's that?" Captain Zain asked.

"We picked him up along the way. He's my chef," Fen replied. "Now, tell me what else needs to be done before we can pack up and head home."

Char traveled out of earshot, but he was glad to have had an excuse to leave. Besides the fact that Captain Zain was extremely intimidating, seeing someone else touch Fen so gently—even if it had just been a healer—had made something ugly and sour erupt inside Char. Worse than sucking on a lemon. And yet, that ugly feeling fought with the butterflies that erupted when Fen said "my chef" in that almost proprietary tone. Char found it far easier to focus on the potential of burnt or trampled potatoes than to try figuring out what the heck was wrong with him. He hurried back to camp and to his fire where he could pretend life was simple again.

Chapter Seven

THE FIRE HAD remained unscathed during the fighting. Char's potatoes needed a few hours to bake, and since the wood or ashes from the fire weren't scattered, he felt safe assuming the potatoes were safe. He did reach into the embers to check one, squeezing gently, which told him the potato was only starting to soften and hadn't been stepped on.

Assured lunch was okay, Char refocused on the rest of his supplies, which hadn't fared as well.

The packs containing the food looked like they had been kicked multiple times. The tops had been forced open and the smaller bags inside tossed about and trampled. One of the bags of dried peas had been opened and scattered everywhere. A bag of dried meat had a muddy footprint on it and looked squashed, but the insides could still be salvaged. The bags of dishes had fared worse, many of the plates broken, the enameled wood not able to hold up to the trampling of booted feet. Silverware was as scattered as the peas, but at least it wasn't broken. Char gathered the food first, checking every bag and making two piles. One for everything that could still be used, and the second for what needed to be thrown away. Once the food was checked, Char moved over to the dishes. Everything not broken that had spilled out he put in a pile to be washed, everything broken he put in a pile to throw out, and he checked through everything still in the bags to make sure he didn't miss anything.

A glance around the camp showed he was alone. The rest of the group were probably still dealing with the aftermath of the fighting. Char had no idea what that entailed, but his assigned kitchen crew was not around. He had gotten used to not having to wash dishes, but he kept his grumbling internal as he gathered the dirty dishes and dumped them into a pot to carry them, found some soap, and headed down to the lake.

But as he started down the hill, he realized he wasn't alone. Three people were near the water's edge, and Char swallowed hard when he realized two were kneeling over the one lying prone in a pool of blood. The two kneeling were healers, their hands glowing green over the body. As he drew closer, Char recognized Clarise. One healer had his hands pressed to her abdomen, the other had one hand on her upper thigh and the other on Clarise's arm.

"Can I—?" Char coughed to clear his throat, his gaze caught on Clarise's pale, clammy skin, so different to the rosy shade of her usual light-brown complexion. "What can I do to help?"

The healer working on her abdomen opened his eyes and glanced over. "Tea, if you have it." He sounded exhausted, his voice thin and reedy, but the green magic coating his hands was strong and even.

"On it," Char replied. He dumped the dishes on the ground—well out of the way of the blood—and took the pot to the lake. Char walked out into the water, away from the churned-up silt on the bank. He gave the pot a quick rinse and then dunked it deep into the water where anything on the surface wouldn't get inside. He also checked he didn't accidentally catch a fish as he pulled the pot out. Then he hurried back to the fire. The pot went into the hottest spot on the grill, and Char tossed on a couple more logs to make the fire burn hotter. Since a watched pot *never* boiled, Char left it to do its thing and returned to his pile of dishes. He found two cups and the diffuser, located where the soap had gotten buried, and returned to the lake to wash them. By the time he returned to the fire, the pot was starting to steam.

The teapot was one of the items that had remained safely packed. Char unearthed it, slipped the diffuser into the slot, and then went digging for the bags of dried tea leaves. At the very bottom of the pack he found the ginseng, which was the best tea for restoring energy. He assumed Fen's group had packed it for exactly that purpose, although in the evenings Char had been serving his own blend of rose and chamomile instead. Char measured the leaves into the diffuser, by which point the water had reached a full boil. He pulled the pot off the heat and left it to cool, keeping an eye on the bubbles and the steam until he was certain he wouldn't burn the leaves. Without a thermometer he couldn't be exact and ensure the tea would retain the health benefits that were best preserved at a precise temperature, but he knew he could get a fairly close estimation. When the water was ready, he filled the teapot, made sure the diffuser was fully immersed, and brought it and the cups over to the healers.

When Char smelled the earthy, slightly bitter notes, and the tea had reached the right shade of tan, he removed the diffuser and poured.

"Here," he told them. The healers each freed a hand to take a steaming cup, both downing the contents immediately despite the heat. Char offered a refill, glad when the healers sipped this time.

"Thanks, that helps," the healer who had requested the tea said. He sounded better, and he smiled slightly.

"How is she?" Char asked. He topped off their cups.

"We got to her in time," the second healer said between sips. "Right now it's mostly meticulous work, tiny internal stitches that take a lot of power and finesse, and attempting to replenish her lost blood. Another twenty minutes and she'll be safe to be moved, which is largely thanks to our boost from the tea. It's delicious."

"I'll have to find out who made the blend and let them know," Char replied. "It's ginseng and honey crystals."

"Ginseng for the energy boost and honey for some sugar, which also helps refuel the body."

"The honey eases the bitter taste of the ginseng too," Char added, shrugging. He knew about the various health benefits of foods and how to best craft a meal for anyone experiencing certain illnesses or difficulties, but that was the end of the overlap between chef's training and a healer's.

They finished the tea and set their mugs aside, waving Char off when he offered another refill. They got back to work, so Char left the teapot nearby and returned to his abandoned pile of dishes.

"There you are!" Ralph called an indeterminant amount of time later. Char looked up from the fork that had a particularly stubborn spot of mud on one tine, and realized he had completely zoned out his surroundings. Sometimes—actually far more often than Char really wanted to admit—the repetitive motions of washing or chopping, or even stirring, sent him to a happy place in his head where swirling thoughts and anxious worries faded away. The soothing abandonment of the world definitely helped him get through difficult times, but it was still abandonment.

Still, there were too many things Char didn't want to think about right now. Clarise, lying in a pool of blood, hurt so badly her healers had parched themselves dry of energy. Fen, his face bruised and swollen, yet still smiling at him as if it didn't hurt. Those damned butterflies that erupted inside Char's stomach every time he thought about Fen's smile shouldn't be anywhere close to the same list, and yet the extreme confusion they caused had Char shying away. And that was besides the fact that Fen was a prince who had no business smiling like that at a lowly chef, even if Char was an Oba-Musen. What Fen hadn't elaborated on was that there was a hierarchy even within the Musen family. Only those who could manifest the passive skill of neutralizing poison *and* were rated tier one after graduation received the Oba prefix, which meant "elder" in the old tongue. However, that designation only meant Char was a really good cook. He wasn't anywhere close to equal to a prince or a commander, and Char therefore shouldn't let the darn butterflies manifest at all.

Yet every time Fen smiled: whoosh and butterflies. Every. Darned. Time.

"I heard you saved our captain," Ralph said as he joined Char at the water's edge. He picked up another fork and started scrubbing. "We really appreciate it, you know."

"He told me who he is, so you don't have to call him captain in front of me," Char replied, finally getting the mud unstuck from the tine.

Ralph nodded and set his cleaned fork aside on the cloth to dry, picking up a spoon next. He was serious, not prone to smiles, yet friendly even though he hated kitchen duty. "You saved our commander then," he replied with a shrug. "Anyway, commander said to hurry you up. Captain Zain wants us moving out within the hour. It's about four days to the city from here, and she wants to use all the daylight we have left. We're packing up the tents, loading up the horses, and putting out fires right now."

"Not with my potatoes in it, they're not!" Char dropped his cleaned fork onto the pile and left Ralph with the rest, which was now only the things he'd used to make tea earlier, and rushed over to the kitchen area. Clarise and the healers were gone and the camp buzzing with activity as the tents were taken down and the horses saddled. Laura was loading Char's pack donkey with the bags from around the fire, which Char saw with a flash of relief was still burning merrily. She had used the mitts to move the grill off to the side to cool.

"Hey!" she called with a smile when Char joined her. "I left that bag for the rest of the dishes. Anything else you need?"

"Just these," Char explained before sticking his hands into the embers and starting to pull out potatoes. He placed them on the grill, which was cool enough it wouldn't continue cooking them and was much better than the ground.

"Yes!" Laura cheered, then yelled over in the direction of the tents: "Hey, guys. Baked potatoes!"

"All right!" Jensen was the first to arrive, followed by everyone else except Fen and Clarise.

"They're hot!" Char yelped when Jensen blithely reached for a potato.

"And I'm starving," Jensen replied with an easy shrug. He pulled his sleeve down over his hand, grabbed a potato, smiled at Char, and then hustled off toward the tents again. The rest of the group followed his example until only three potatoes remained.

"Where's Fen?" Char asked, wondering what to do with the two extras.

"Behind you," Fen said. "I heard there were potatoes, so I came over."

Fen and Captain Zain joined Char and Laura next to the fire. Laura was holding her potato with her sleeve over her hand, gently blowing on one of the rounded ends, although she nodded to her commanding officers.

"It's just plain potato. Not even any salt. I'm not sure it's fully cooked in the middle. And it's covered in ash, too." Char wrung his hands, unhappy he was inadvertently serving such a lackluster meal.

"It's exactly what we need right now. Nothing fiddly, simple and filling. Much better than jerky I promise you," Fen said as he yanked down his sleeve and grabbed a potato. "Clarise won't be up to eating hers. Zain, go ahead. And Char, the last one is yours I believe?"

Char nodded, taking one in his bare hand. Zain's left eyebrow lifted, and she shot Fen a look Char couldn't interpret. She had changed out of her armor into a tunic and breeches and slipped her sleeve over her hand to take the last potato.

The potato was too hot for even Char to eat, so he used his free hand to tip the remaining water from the pot he had used to make tea over the fire, dousing it and sending up a plume of smoke. He brought the emptied pot down to the lake for Ralph to use to load all the cleaned dishes into, and by the time they both returned to Laura and the donkey to load the last supplies, the potatoes were cool enough to eat.

Fluffy, but dry and definitely needing seasoning, the potato somehow still tasted delicious. It had been a long time since breakfast, and a fraught day, so perhaps that was why Char kept taking bites even though lacking flavor. At least the ash provided a nice grilled flavor to offset the otherwise bland food. All too soon, the potato was gone.

"Right," Zain said, dusting off her hands against her hips. "Let's mount up and move out."

Laura finished loading the last of the supplies onto the donkey. Char took the lead from her and headed over to the horses, finding his pony easily since it only had the one pack behind the saddle. Also, his pony was smaller than the warhorses, which helped. He mounted, secured the lead, and joined the group as Fen waved them forward, gladly leaving behind the lake and their completed mission. They would meet up with Zain's larger group and then continue into Toval.

Chapter Eight

RAIN HAD BEEN falling the last four hours, beating heavily on Char's soaked head and turning the roads to mush. His pony let out another unhappy whinny, echoed by the larger horses around them, but continued plodding gamely on. Lightning flashed, the bolt slashing across the faraway horizon, the boom of thunder muffled by the distance. And still, it poured.

Despite being only late afternoon, the sky was dark and the surroundings misty and shadowed. Char could barely see a few feet in front of his pony's nose, and he sincerely hoped Fen and Zain, up at the front of their group, knew where they were going.

Suddenly a massive wall rose out of the gloom, towering over them by at least three stories. They rode parallel to it for a while, which was a relief since it helped cut the wind. Eventually they reached a gate set into the wall. People ran out to open the gate and they rode through a lengthy stone-flagged tunnel, horseshoes ringing against the stone and echoing through the space. They emerged in a courtyard where they were immediately swarmed by even more people. Someone untied the donkey's lead and took the pony's reins from Char. He dismounted and grabbed his bag, but Char had no idea where he was or where he was supposed to go. He awkwardly stood in the courtyard, a flurry of activity going on around him, rain beating down on his head, and wondering what he should do.

"Char!" The call, muffled by rain and distance, was definitely Fen's voice. "Char, where are you?"

"Here!" Char yelled back, waving his hand over his head and hoping wherever Fen was he'd see.

"There you are." Fen materialized out of the gloom at Char's side. "Indications are the weather isn't going to improve any time soon. Why don't you bed down with us tonight, and I'll bring you over to the palace in the morning?"

"We're in Etoval?" Char asked, surprised. Yes, the weather was terrible, but surely he wouldn't have missed riding through the massive capital city.

"In the military complex north of the city. About a ten-minute ride away. Come on, let's get out of the rain."

Char followed Fen closely, afraid to lose sight of him in the bustle and the poor visibility. The courtyard was surrounded by buildings on the three sides that weren't the gate and wall. Fen went to the right, where a path led deeper into the complex. The tall buildings on either side helped keep more of the rain off, which was nice. When they reached another courtyard, they dashed across through the rain. Then, they arrived at a path heading left, leading toward the middle of the complex and no longer following the line of the wall.

"This place is like a maze," Char muttered, glancing around as they reached a third courtyard. Fen grinned over his shoulder at Char, the flash of his white teeth visible even in the rain-soaked gloom, and finally led Char into a building.

"We own the first two floors," Fen explained as they both stood in the entryway, dripping water onto the flagstones. "The rest of the building has a separate entrance. This way."

Fen led the way out of the entry and into a massive common room. Deep, comfortable-looking couches were scattered around the space, many of them circled around the massive fireplace dominating the right-hand wall. There were fewer tables, but they were placed strategically around the couches. The left-hand wall contained a fully stocked bar. Across the room was a long hallway, doorways dotting either side. Fen went all the way to the end where the hall terminated at a closed set of double doors. A staircase going up was to the left, and Fen opened the door on the right to reveal a bedroom.

"This room is currently empty, so you can use it tonight," Fen explained. "Drop your bag off. There should be a robe hanging in one of the closets. Grab that, and I'll show you the bathing facility."

Since Char was shivering and still dripping, that sounded like a marvelous idea. The room had two full beds pushed against opposite walls with two dressers between them underneath the window. Small blanket trunks sat at the foot of each bed, next to which each had an armor and weapons stand. Against the wall on opposite sides of the door were two ceiling-height wardrobes. Char left his bag on the floor, pulled open one of the wardrobe doors, and found a blue robe hanging inside amid a lot of empty hangers. He returned to the hallway in time to see Fen jog down the stairs holding a green robe.

"This way," he said, going back down the hall until they were at the closed door closest to the common room. The door opened into a changing room with cubbies lining the walls. Each cubby had hooks at the top and a seat with a drawer at the bottom. Fen hung his robe on one hook and pulled his shirt over his head. Char gulped and spun around, picking a random cubby on the other side of the room. He stripped quickly, dragging his sodden, clinging clothes away from his skin, and left them hanging on the hooks to start drying. He quickly donned the robe and turned around to find Fen waiting for him, wrapped in the green robe.

"Is there a separate room for women?" Char asked, wondering about the lack of privacy.

"It's across the hall. One door down are the water closets, men's on this side, women's on the other." He pushed open the door on the far side of the room, revealing exactly as Char feared: a communal shower area.

Oddly, though, as Char took in the tiled space, he noticed there weren't any pumps or tubs, just shower heads and spigots. "You have running water?" Char asked, awed. He had heard it existed but had never seen it before.

"The palace was retrofitted about ten years ago. We're only halfway through with the military complex, but another building is converted every year. Most of the city hasn't made the transition since it's expensive and time consuming, but the palace is offering subsidies to help. It's healthier to bring water into the city from the aquifers, and pump the used water out into the southern ravines, than to have wells in proximity to outhouses. We've already reduced the number of cholera outbreaks, which allows the city healers to focus on other, less serious issues, which then continues to improve health overall." He paused and shrugged sheepishly. "Sorry, convincing the military complex to switch over was a pet project of mine." His hands went to the belt of his robe, and Char's cheeks heated, those darned butterflies surging. Fen didn't appear to be the least bit self-conscious. "Left handle is hot, right is cold. Use them both to find a temperature you like. Soap's in the pump bottles on the wall." Fen continued as Char looked away, focusing on his own spigot.

A hook was set into the wall on either side of the handles. Above the handles three bottles hung from brackets, shampoo, conditioner, and soap, according to the labels. Char let out a breath and pulled off his robe, then hung it up. He fiddled with the handles, yelping when he got sprayed by freezing water.

Fen chuckled, and Char accidentally looked over, after which he was glad for the cold as it prevented his body from reacting the way the immediate roaring in Char's head wanted it to. Fen's back was to Char, hard muscles outlined by dripping water, drawing the eye down to firm buttocks and long legs. Char refocused his attention on the wall in front of him, turning the knobs until the water warmed to comfortable levels, then luxuriating in the chance to finally feel warm for the first time all afternoon and telling his body to get a grip on reality. He soaped up quickly; the faster he was done with the shower, the faster he was away from a naked Fen.

Char really didn't know what was wrong with him. He was thinking of Fen the same way he thought of making fresh chicken stock, and never before had he conflated food with sex. Never before had another person distracted him from cooking quite like Fen. His feelings weren't appropriate, and Char honestly didn't know what the best thing to do would be. He wasn't interested in other humans in that way often; he'd had sex before, but all his previous partners had fallen short in comparison to spending time in the kitchen and had eventually left him. Char knew where his thoughts would normally be after being presented with the novelty of running water. So many recipes would be made easier thanks to having it, and the cleanup afterward would take half the time and effort. And yet the image of water dripping down Fen's skin kept reappearing.

Char rinsed the last of the soap off and turned off the taps, glad to feel clean for the first time since embarking on the journey into the mountains far too many days ago. He was warmed through too. He looked around, carefully not glancing in Fen's direction, and found a stack of folded towels tucked into a niche next to the door. Char took one and dried off, slipped back into his robe, and gladly returned to the changing room.

"Hey!" Laurence called, smiling at Char from where he was unlacing his boots, sitting in one of the cubbies. "I'm glad someone managed to bring you here. You ought to stay permanently, you know."

Glad for any distraction that yanked his mind away from Fen, still naked and dripping in the other room, Char focused on Laurence.

"I don't know how much work you'd have for me here," Char admitted. "Besides, my cousin has a position waiting for me."

"Family is important," Laurence replied with a nod. He dropped his boots into the drawer and stood to take his shirt off. "Anyway, dirty towel drop is that bin," he pointed to an empty box pushed into a spot on the wall without any cubbies. "The mob of us should be descending on the baths any moment, so you should get out of here before this place gets inundated."

"Thanks," Char said. He went to his cubby to retrieve his damp and, quite frankly, *dank* clothes.

Fen emerged, thankfully robed, as Char was checking he had gotten everything.

"Dinner is going to be delivered to the common area in about an hour," Fen called to Char as he nodded hello to Laurence and went to his own cubby. "Please come join us. And then seven o'clock in the morning to head over to the palace?"

"That works for me. Thanks." Char replied. He escaped into the hallway, which was now filled with the boisterous, welcoming noise of the entire company. They called out to him, and Char waved hello in response, but Char wanted to return to the room Fen allotted him where he didn't have to think for a while. He needed to clear his head, adjust his mental balance back to where it should be, and return exclusively to the world of cooking where he belonged.

A servant was waiting just outside the door, a basket in his hands. "Sir, I made one of the beds and laid out a set of clean clothes for you. If you want to give me anything that needs washing, I'll have it returned to you first thing in the morning.

"That would be amazing." Char grinned at him, thankful he wouldn't be appearing in Terrance's kitchen smelling like he had just spent weeks in the woods. "We can start with these," Char continued, indicating his wet clothes. The servant held out the basket and Char deposited everything inside. He went into his room, where his bag had been placed on top of the blanket chest at the end of a bed that was now neatly made with sheets, pillows, and blankets, and started pulling out the rest of his dirty, travel-stained clothes. Everything went into the basket. Char double-checked he hadn't missed anything and then went over to the other, unmade bed where a set of brown pants and a loose white shirt had been laid out.

"Whose are these?" he asked.

"They're from the general stock," the servant replied. "Everyone who lives here is outfitted from there; since you're living here tonight, you can borrow the clothes while I get yours washed. Let me know if you need anything else," he added before leaving. Char let out a heavy breath as the servant shut the door behind him.

Char collapsed onto his bed and sighed again. He would get dressed in a moment and head out to the common room to eat, but first he had to clear his mind. Any thoughts of Fen needed to go into a locked box where he could forget about them. Char focused on daydreams of what working in Terrance's kitchen would be like, wishing that might be enough to banish Fen from the forefront of his mind. The palace must serve amazing food, with access to unique ingredients Char had never had the opportunity to work with. Banquets, luxuries, and a chance to work with other high-level chefs. Learning new recipes, new techniques; Char couldn't wait. He knew it would be amazing, and the morning couldn't come soon enough.

Chapter Nine

"I WANT TO show you something."

Char froze, his face stretched in a yawn, his body only halfway into the hallway as he had been in the process of leaving his room. He snapped his mouth shut, continuing out and closing the door of the very comfortable room behind him, then turned to look at Fen where he was leaning against the banister.

"Show me what?" Char asked. It was six thirty in the morning. If Char were working the morning shift, he would already be up and elbow-deep in bread flour and eggs, but after the last few weeks of hard travel, sleeping in had been a luxury. Sometime in the night his clothes had been returned, neatly stacked in folded piles on the bed he wasn't using. This morning, he changed into a set of his own clothes, packed everything else away, and was ready to see Terrance.

"Something to think about while you're at the palace kitchen," Fen explained cryptically. He gripped the handles of the closed double doors and pushed them open, revealing a massive room easily the same size as the entire building behind them. To the left were at least a dozen dusty four- to eight-seater tables, the chairs upside down on top. Two more sets of double doors were located in the wall past the tables, also closed. Char looked and realized the doors he and Fen were standing in were also paired by another set in the same wall, so Char assumed four bunkhouses fed into this space. The wall directly across from Char was entirely windows, with the final set of glassed double doors leading out into some sort of courtyard.

To the right—Char sucked in a shocked breath.

The kitchen was enormous, spanning the entire wall. Two huge sinks were installed on either side. The left one, located near a massive cabinet containing more pots and pans of every shape and size than Char could ever dream of, was clearly meant for dishwashing. The other sink was located near what appeared to be a proper—meaning magic-produced—cold and ice box, so was obviously for preparing food. Along the back wall, metal countertops for food prep spanned the space between the sinks, and upper shelves filled with serving dishes were hung above the long counter.

A massive island was placed between the tables to the left and the sink to the right. Char crept closer, knowing his mouth was hanging open but not caring. This closer side of the island was clearly for serving. Featuring a long flat space with indentations for warming candles or ice, there were also drawers underneath, no doubt containing various stands for different sized chafing dishes.

Char reached the other side of the island and stopped dead. The entire span was stove. Dozens of burners of different sizes, grills, warming plates, even a dipped space for a wok. Below that were oven doors the entire length, each one meant for different heats depending on how close or how far from three separate spots to build a fire. Though everything was coated in a thick layer of gray dust, it was so beautiful.

"There are only about a hundred to a hundred fifty royal guards on staff, plus about another fifty servants," Fen explained. "A lot of the time we're off on missions, so that number is constantly fluctuating. We're an unruly bunch too. Finding a cook willing to stay here in the stark military complex with only us for company—and only while we're actually in residence—has proven impossible. I know you have a job in the palace waiting for you with your cousin," Fen added quickly. "However, I wanted you to know if you were interested, this kitchen could be yours. There would be a food budget to stick to, but you would make all culinary decisions here."

A dream kitchen and a dream job. Char couldn't imagine why anyone would turn it down. Except for a chance to work in the palace, of course. Here, Char would be alone, using only his own skills. In the palace, he could learn from other masters. That wasn't an opportunity he could afford to pass up.

"Let's head over to the palace so you can meet your cousin," Fen continued, clearly understanding Char couldn't give him an answer yet. "All I wanted was for you to know you have options."

Char had to clear his throat to find his voice. "I appreciate it." He followed Fen back out of the kitchen, tearing his eyes away as Fen closed the doors again. They went down the hallway and through the common room, empty this early in the morning.

"Today is a day off for everyone who was out at the lake with us. Everyone else should be at the main mess getting breakfast," Fen explained as they walked through the silence of couches and low tables that last night had been full of boisterous excitement ringing from every corner.

They went outside and retraced their path between the buildings and across courtyards until they reached the main gate. A horse and Char's pony were waiting for them, saddled and ready to go. Char secured his bag and mounted, following Fen through the long tunnel under the wall and then outside.

With the sun shining, Char could see a lot better today than yesterday. The walls were made of gigantic stone blocks, dark gray and sturdy. Outside, fields of grass were dotted with what Char thought were flocks of goats and sheep, likely why the grass was short. The road out of the gate was cobbled, not that Char had noticed last night. They rode through the fields until it forked, one heading into the forest where they must have come from last night, the other they took now.

Fen had said it was only a ten-minute ride to the city. Within five minutes, Char could see the smoke rising from the chimneys and the outer wall, which looked to be made of more gigantic gray stone. The city was on a hill, sprawling down into the grassland below, and at the very top of the hill were the spires and towers of the palace. The road forked again, one going downward to what was probably the main gates into the city. They went left, away from the main gates and heading up the hill while still angling toward the city.

"We're going to the private entrance for the palace residents," Fen explained as they approached a large gate heavily manned by guards. They caught sight of Fen from a distance, so the gate was already raised when they arrived. Fen and Char didn't slow as they trotted under the wall and into the complex. A hostler and a bevy of servants met them inside. Char took his bag but left his pony to the hostler.

"Head Chef Musen is expecting him," Fen explained to one of the servants. "Can you show him the way there?"

"Yes, Your Highness," the servant replied, bowing.

"I'm sure I'll see you around," Fen said to Char. "So, I won't say goodbye. Good luck though." He smiled and then spun to the group of people fighting for his attention.

Char let out a breath and turned away, following the servant across the courtyard, purposefully not looking back to get one last look at Fen. They didn't travel too far. What looked like warehouses surrounded the left side of the courtyard. The servant took a path between two of them, which let out into a smaller yard with a set of wide double doors set into the wall at the foot of one of the soaring towers. The doors were open, letting the clack and clang of pots and pans, the rhythmic thumps of chopping, and the general bustle of a lot of people inside flow outside. It already sounded wonderful; so much going on, and so much to therefore learn.

Inside, the servant paused, which gave Char a chance to look around. If Fen's kitchen from the morning had been impressive, this was magnificent. Triple the size, three massive islands, and the walls completely enclosed in countertops, aside from the left wall which was half cold box, and half ice box, and the right wall, which was entirely ovens and stovetops. The entire wall! Every flat surface and each of the six sinks had people working feverishly. The atmosphere was frenetic though. No one was smiling, but it wasn't because they were focused. They were stressed, which made Char frown too. Cooking ought to be fun—hard work, yes, but still fun.

"What?" someone snapped at the servant, skidding to a stop in front of them, hands full of dirty dishes.

"Chef Musen is expecting him," the servant explained, apparently unfazed by the rudeness.

"Right." He left the dishes on an already overfilled counter next to one of the sinks where someone was busy scrubbing. "This way."

He led them through the bustle, deftly avoiding everyone working. Char wended past as well, catching sight of fish, meats of all kinds, so many vegetables being prepared in dozens of ways, and that was as amazing as Char had hoped. These were experts at their craft, with so much to learn and so many people to learn from. The opportunities in the room that Char could see were nearly endless. And yet, no one was smiling.

"Chef," the man said, knocking on the jamb of a doorway leading into a private office.

"I'm busy," Terrance snapped. "What do you need now?"

"Visitor here for you?" the man answered before backing away and returning to the bustle.

Char stepped into the doorway, looking into an office with a large desk covered in paperwork, the walls full of shelves and cabinets.

Terrance stood from behind the desk, appearing behind a stack of papers. He was scowling, his eyes blazing with fury until he caught sight of Char.

"Charmaine! I was getting worried!" he exclaimed, scowl fading as he hurried around the desk with his arms out. He pulled Char into a hug. "I expected you last week." Terrance was about fifteen years older than Char. They shared the same deep-black hair, but the similarities ended there. Where Char's eyes were dark blue, Terrance's were brown, and Terrance was a few inches taller, with his mother's nose. They were blood related through their fathers.

"It took a little longer than expected to cross the mountain," Char explained. "But I'm here now. This is a very interesting kitchen."

Terrance nodded. "It's a great place for an Oba-Musen to work. Easy. Let me show you around."

He slipped past Char and led the way into the kitchen. "Food preparation is this side of the kitchen," he explained, heading to the side of the room where the cold boxes were. "Cleaning meat, washing vegetables, any peeling. Once it's ready, it goes to the center stations where it's chopped, stuffed, kneaded, and marinated. On this side is where the cooking happens," he continued, going over to the ovens and stovetops. Terrance idly picked up a spoon and stirred one of the sauces bubbling there—a thick marinara if the sharp scent of acidic tomatoes and fragrant garlic that met Char's nose was correct—after which he flipped a tag hanging from the pot's handle so it showed blue, rather than the red from before. "Our job is simple. They hired me—and you—to ensure no food that ever leaves this kitchen is poisoned. We are required to stir, baste, or knead every single item cooked. I marked that sauce as completed, so it can now be served." He returned to his office, leaning against a corner of his desk and grinning at Char. "What do you think? Nice, easy work for really good pay. I take care of a lot of the paperwork for ordering and planning, so it's not like I'm freeloading here."

"When do you cook?" Char asked. There were so many helpers, with every space out there filled, and Char was starting to get a sinking feeling in the pit of his stomach.

Terrance shrugged. "If the king orders something particular, I might take the lead on the preparation, but that's the beauty of working in this kitchen. We have other people to handle the drudgery. Now with you here, the mundane tasks will be halved!"

Char kept his mouth shut on the thoughts furiously swirling inside. They were chefs, not paper pushers! And their magical gifts weren't for stirring sauces, of which Terrance hadn't even tasted before marking ready to serve! Char wanted to cook, not sit around waiting for someone else to do the work. If he stayed here, Char knew he would go crazy. Luckily, he had another option. A very welcoming kitchen that was all his own.

"Terr, I'm sorry. I came to let you know I made it to the city, and to decline your offer of employment. I've been asked to become a private chef, running my own kitchen. It's an opportunity I have to take."

Terrance looked shocked, his jaw hanging open, as if he couldn't imagine Char saying no to a lazy job as a chef where he didn't have to actually do any real work.

"I'm a head chef at twenty-six," Char continued, grinning. "Even for an Oba-Musen, that's young."

Terrance shut his mouth and let out a heavy sigh. "Yes, that's certainly true. Very prestigious. Well, if you change your mind or this job doesn't work out, you'll always have a position here." He held out his arms, pulling Char into another hug. "I am glad you made it to Etoval safely. Be sure to come visit on occasion."

"Of course. Thank you, Terrance."

Char left, wending his way through the bustle of the kitchen and back out into the small courtyard. Once outside, he let out a heavy breath, trying to let the weight of the unhappiness within that kitchen fall away. Fen must have known Char wouldn't be happy working with Terrance—the timing of his offer of the kitchen in the barracks was a little too pointed—but Char had loved that kitchen. In the end, the decision was easy. Yes, Char would have to figure out his feelings for Fen, and how to suppress them despite continued close proximity, but in the end the draw of that kitchen won.

And, perhaps, the draw of being able to continue cooking for Fen won as well.

Char hurried along the path between the warehouses, returning to the courtyard with the gate. Fen would have to return to the military complex at some point, so Char would wait for him in the yard to let him know Char was happy to be his chef again.

Interlude

FEN PUSHED OPEN the dining room door and walked inside, knowing this early in the morning everyone would be sitting down to breakfast.

"Uh-oh. He's got his man-on-a-mission face on." Braxton sniggered and waved his fork in Fen's direction in hello.

Mother looked up and patted her lips with her napkin as she studied him. She set the napkin aside and smiled. "That's the face all my children make when they've fallen in love. Tell me who the lucky man is, dear."

"Ooh. Someone's fallen in love?" Braxton asked, catcalling and laughing.

"Shut up, Braxton," Fen snapped, rolling his eyes and wishing his perennial request to have Brax's lips sewn shut would be approved. He turned to Father, who was buried behind a cup of tea. "I found a chef for the royal forces. Can you release the funds held for the kitchen there?"

"Found how?" Ayer asked, sounding skeptical. "Don't tell me you kidnapped someone to force them to take that post."

"Ha ha, very funny," Fen growled, wishing the crown prince would get strangled by his crown. He focused on Father, hoping the rest of his siblings would keep their mouths shut. "You remember we chose to target the Blood Lions mercenary group because they have a habit of pillaging our border towns whenever they run low on funds?" Which was often because their leader, Greath, spent money on ridiculous things all the time. "He hired a private chef for the trip to the lake. I decided not to kill him."

"How wonderful," Mother said with a happy sigh. "When do I get to meet him?"

"At least tell us his name," Shairon added. She was wiping her oldest son's face, the three-year-old somehow managing to get more food on himself than into his mouth. Ayer's oldest brat was six and she was copying Mother, primly patting her mouth with her napkin.

"Charmaine Oba-Musen," Fen replied.

Father put his teacup down. "You're stealing my new chef?"

"A Musen?" Braxten added, sniggering. "If he's anything like that fop we've currently got in our kitchen, he's no catch even if he can cook."

"He's nothing like his cousin," Fen snapped. "And yes, I'm stealing him. He's touring the palace kitchen right now, but knowing him, he'll be horrified. I offered him the job in my kitchen this morning. He was practically drooling at the prospect, so I'm certain he'll say no to his cousin and come work for me instead."

"Darling, sit down and tell us about him," Mother insisted, waving toward an open seat. Fen sat and waited while a servant poured him tea and set a plate in front of him. Pancakes with macerated strawberries and fresh syrup, and at the first bite Fen knew if Char had made this dish it would be so much better. Something was missing. Fen couldn't put his finger on what, but he bet Char would take one bite and be able to list off everything wrong.

The poor guy hadn't cooked the last four days, Zain's soldiers taking over the chore. They had moved too quickly to do more than light a fire briefly to heat things, although Fen had seen Char surreptitiously sneaking dashes of salt or giving a skillet a flip. Even last night with the dinner delivered from the main dining hall in the military complex, Fen had watched Char eat and try to keep the grimace from his face. The poor guy could not conceal anything inside; his face revealed exactly what he was thinking every time. That was one of the many things that made him so cute.

"Will you approve the kitchen expenses?" Fen asked.

Father sighed. "If he does choose to work for you, I'll release the funds." He took a sip of tea, then set it aside. "Tell me about the rest of the trip. I've read the reports you and Captain Zain sent ahead, but your missive implied something you couldn't put into writing?"

Fen put his silverware down. "One of my vetted soldiers tried to poison us all after we took out Greath. I'm only here because Char was cooking, and the poison was neutralized. My soldier confessed before she killed herself. She said, and I quote, 'Randolph says hi.'"

"Shit." Ayer banged his fist on the table.

"Wasn't Uncle Randolph finally killed three years ago in the battle at Oaker?" Shairon asked.

"I took his head off myself," Braxton answered. "Unless he has an identical twin somewhere, the bastard is dead."

"Randolph was not a twin and was my only sibling with any sort of vendetta against the crown," Father replied. He rubbed his eyes with one hand, letting out a sigh. "But he had supporters, some of whom were located in Namin so we couldn't arrest them. Do you have any idea how they turned your soldier, or whether anyone else has been compromised?"

"Not yet, but Jensen is looking into it. I know I can trust him, and all Char cares about is making good food. I can trust him too, even if I found him with Greath."

"Is that all he cares about?" Mother asked. "Does he return your feelings?"

"Mother!" Braxton hissed. "We're talking about that bastard Randolph returning from the dead! Fenwick's romance isn't important right now."

She gave Brax *the look*, and he snapped his mouth shut. "Of course it matters. Fen's chef is in a unique position to influence or even to attack. Because Fen's feelings will make him lower his guard; plus, a chef can easily slip things into food. Charmaine will be approached. They will try to bribe him, threaten him, or otherwise force him to hurt Fen because of his special access. So, does he return your feelings enough to be trusted when that happens?"

"You're right that Char is a target who needs to be protected, but he's really strong. It doesn't matter whether he returns my feelings, although I hope he does. He's stubborn and once he's given his loyalty, it's unwavering. It'll take something big to discombobulate him. I'm working to ensure they don't have easy access either. He's safe in the military complex where someone will be with him at all times, and if he leaves, it will be with a guard."

"And in the meantime, Ayer and I will leverage our resources to see if we can figure out this new conspiracy," Father said, shaking his head and sighing. "I had hoped my brother's jealous rage had subsided with his death."

"I suspect Namin has been fermenting it," Ayer added with his own sigh. "Did you ever figure out why that group of mercenaries was hired? Did you get anything out of Prince Clament?"

"He recognized me immediately, so he never said what the final orders were. We've searched his belongings, and he's sitting in prison right now. Hopefully that will soften him up. I'll let you know."

"*I'll* let you know," Braxton cut in. "He's under my care now."

"Then he'll definitely talk, if only not to see your ugly face anymore," Fen replied, sniggering.

"Boys." Mother shot them both a look, but then her smile softened and turned seraphic. "While you wait for the information, you can spend time wooing your chef." She might pretend to be airheaded or only interested in her children's love lives, but behind that innocent look was a shrewd and calculating mind.

"Mother," Fen said in a drawn-out groan, trying to focus his attention on his breakfast.

Braxton snorted out a laugh. "Yes, tell us all about wooing your chef while Mother starts planning your wedding."

"Don't joke, Brax," Fen snapped in reply. "Now that I've got a person I'm interested in, that leaves only you for Mother to matchmake for. You ready to dance with Baroness Uthromis again?"

Brax cringed. "Not a chance. I like having toes attached to my feet, and I like being single." He looked at Mother pleadingly. "I really like being single."

Satisfied the conversation had been diverted from his own budding romance, particularly since the redirection was at Brax's expense, Fen returned to his pancakes.

He finally escaped an hour later and made his way back through the castle to the private entrance where his horse would be waiting. His heart was beating in his throat as he approached, and he immediately scanned the yard. At first, Fen didn't see Char. A delivery wagon was being unloaded in the middle of the yard, blocking his view. But then he caught sight of a flash of black hair and saw Char leaning against the wall, out of the way. Heart still thumping a touch too hard, Char headed in his direction.

"Everything okay?" Fen asked.

Char looked up at Fen and sighed. "Is your offer of employment still available?"

"Yes. Would you like to be the chef of the royal guard complex?" Fen asked.

"I would. Thank you."

Char smiled at him, and Fen had to swallow down his first, but not publicly appropriate, reaction. Relief flooded his body, and his heart stopped thudding with worry. Char would be safe and nearby, and Fen would have plenty of time to gently woo this lovely man.

"Shall we return so you can conduct an inventory of what your new kitchen has and make a list of everything you need?" Fen asked.

"I'd like that." Char was still smiling, but it brightened a little more at Fen's words.

Fen waved to the waiting hostler to ask for their horses to be brought. "Then let's go get started."

Chapter Ten

A SHOUT OF laughter came from one of the tables by the windows. Char looked up, already smiling, to watch the group of four enjoying their breakfasts. The past three months of long hours and sleepless nights, trial and error, and a lot of planning had transformed the place. The dust was long gone, the cold and ice boxes and pantry fully stocked, and all the neglected cookware shined. The kitchen had really only been fully operational for the last two weeks, although Char had done his best to cook in the meantime as he finished all the setup. Ensuring he had all the proper cooking and serving items, obtaining regular vendors to send him new stock, organizing help, and all the other little things that had to been done had seemed endless at first. He had been so busy, he had barely seen Fen, which had helped keep him focused on the multitude of tasks at hand, even if that absence twisted something painful inside whenever Char thought about it. Finally, though, Char could say all his preparations, all the failures and successes of setting up a brand-new kitchen for the very first time, had been successful. He had happy diners and a good process down for cooking and serving, and he finally felt he could settle in to this new life he had chosen for himself.

Char lifted a pan off the burner, flicked his wrist, and the omelet inside flipped perfectly, landing back in the pan without even a wrinkle in the egg. He added shredded cheddar and looked up at the woman waiting on the other side of the island.

"Veggies?" he asked.

She nodded. "Yes, please."

Char added a generous scoop of sautéed vegetables—mushrooms, onions, red, yellow, and green peppers, and spinach—carefully folded the delicate egg in half to cover the veggies and cheese, and turned the burner down to low to give the cheese a chance to melt and incorporate with the vegetables. The serving side of the island was full of food too. Fresh bagels and sliced bread, blueberry and cranberry muffins—all of which he had made this morning—homemade jams—which he had been bottling all summer in between everything else he had worked on—and his carefully curated purchases of cream cheese and lox. He had a fresh berry salad and some yogurt set out as well. He only did individual orders for omelets on rare occasions like this morning, when he knew the diners would trickle in throughout the designated breakfast hours between six and ten in the morning. Some mealtimes it was all Char could do to keep the serving platters full, but today was morning drill, so only those with evening shifts who were exempt came down for breakfast. The herd of locusts that comprised the postdrill fighters would descend on the muffins around eleven, which was why Char was keeping an eye on the double batch currently in the oven.

They would eat double portions when lunch opened an hour from then, so the respite was short-lived.

Char slid the finished omelet onto the outheld plate and set the pan aside on a cool burner. He turned his burner off. No one else was in line, so Char went over to where the rolls for lunch were proofing under a cloth. They had risen nicely, plump and about the size of Char's palm, so he removed the cloths and slotted the trays into racks in the oven Char had designated for bread. A glance at the clock on the wall said it was 8:15. He would take them out when they had doubled in size, had turned golden brown, and developed a firm crust and chewy internal texture, which was about twenty minutes. He couldn't fit all 300 rolls into the one oven, of course, but they would all be ready to eat by the time the kitchen opened for lunch.

One task done, Char went to check on how today's assigned helpers were doing. Each of the four barracks supplied one worker each meal to help Char out. Two were currently busy scrubbing the ever-present pile of dirty dishes, but he had two more working as sous chefs to help prepare lunch. Warren was tasked with zesting and juicing about a hundred oranges, while Marcus was peeling and grating an equal amount of ginger. Both were doing well enough, but they weren't trained to be sous chefs; Char could see the inconsistencies in their work. Still, help was help. As he had quickly learned, there was no way Char could handle the entire kitchen without them.

He moved over to his own cutting board where he was almost done slicing more red, yellow, and green peppers. The colorful strips would balance nicely with the chicken, cauliflower, broccoli, carrots, and mushrooms he also still needed to prepare for the chicken stir-fry in an orange-ginger glaze he was making for lunch. He had made the rotini earlier at the same time as the bread, so at least that was ready to go, and the rolls were cooking. He wasn't behind schedule, per se, just wishing he had a few more pairs of hands.

Char had finished the peppers and moved on to the cauliflower when a group of two walked in, grabbing plates and waiting expectantly. Char abandoned his vegetables and went to the other counter to start cracking eggs.

Heat the pan on medium with a large pad of butter melting inside. Three eggs, a dash of milk, a dash of salt, and a couple twirls of a pepper mill, then beat with a whisk. Pour over the melted butter, then use a spatula to carefully lift the edges so the liquid could drain underneath. A flip, then cheese, a fold, and done. Repeat, the second one with veggies added to the cheese, and Char was setting the pan aside in record time.

He pulled the muffins out of the oven and set them on a cooling rack, checked on the rolls—which needed another two minutes judging by their too-pale color—and returned to his cutting board until another diner entered the room.

He loved being this busy though. Constantly moving around the kitchen, getting to work on different projects, and the autonomy to meal plan however he wanted; no other kitchen allowed for that freedom. In all his previous jobs Char had been tethered to one station doing the exact same task over and over day after day.

The lunch rush came and went, the stir fry vanishing quickly, and as the quiet returned, Char focused his attention to marinating steak rounds. Ralph and Isa were on dinner duty, and one was peeling potatoes while the other snapped the tips off green beans.

And then Fen walked into the room, and the Zen calm Char had been enjoying vanished like a balloon popping. Three months and those darned butterflies were still a persistent menace. The memory of Fen, naked in the shower liked to pop up at inconvenient moments. Even his smile reminded Char of all the times Fen had pulled Char aside for a private chat—just the two of them standing close, heads bent together—all those times in the forest.

"Hey, Char, can I steal you for a second?" Fen asked.

Char schooled his face into nonchalance, since Fen really didn't need to know how Char's heart jumped at those words. Char's reactions to Fen were beyond ridiculous, and he had no wish to burden Fen with this insanity. Char would get over it eventually; he was certain. He rinsed his hands at the sink and walked around the island to Fen's side. "Sure. What do you need?"

Fen waved behind him, and Jensen walked up, tugging along a teenager who looked sullen and very unhappy to be there.

"This is Karl. We caught him with his hand in Jensen's pocket last week while we were helping with a patrol in the city market. Military court procedure is to sentence anyone caught committing a nonviolent crime against one of the guard groups to serve their time in some sort of support capacity to the group they slighted. Karl was sentenced to six months with us. Problem is, he's as bad with swords, running, and pretty much everything military-related as he is at pickpocketing. I was hoping you could take him under your wing instead?"

The sullen look was replaced by shock as Karl stared at Fen. He was maybe sixteen years old and definitely too skinny. He was dressed in the standard daytime fare given to everyone working for the royal guard—

brown pants and a white shirt—but the white did nothing for his skin tone. He had lank brown hair, but striking gold-brown eyes that would serve him well when he grew up a little more. Poor kid looked washed out, tired, and defeated, once the façade of angry teen was stripped away.

Somehow, Fen had heard Char's inner monologue wishing for more help and had delivered. The slight upturn of his lips said Fen knew exactly what Char was thinking, and that he was happy to have a solution to offer, at least for the next six months.

"I'm sure I can find work for him. Let me get him an apron, and he can help Ralph with the potatoes."

"Yes!" Ralph hissed under his breath.

The apron Char pulled out of the closet hung down to Karl's knees, but it would protect him so Char left it. He waved toward the sink and draining board where Ralph was working.

"You take this brush here and use it to remove any dirt left behind on the skin," Char explained, demonstrating on one of the potatoes for Karl. "You don't need to push hard, just get any clumps off for Ralph to peel. When you're done with the potatoes, you can start on cleaning the mushrooms." He pointed to the basket of baby bellas on the draining board next to the box of potatoes. "It's the same brush, just be a little gentler. You'll get the hang of it," Char finished, handing over the brush and letting Karl get to work. The sullen look was back, but he took the brush from Char and started scrubbing.

Fen hadn't left. Even while focusing on Karl, Char had felt Fen's eyes on his back like twin foxes focused on a bunny. Char didn't mind the intensity or the attention, but he knew he ought to. Had any of his previous acquaintances concentrated so exclusively on Char like that, distracting him from his cooking, Char would have been furious. Yet, when Fen's presence filled the room, Char wanted to baste himself in it as if he were a turkey roasting in the oven. Rather than returning to building his marinade, Char helplessly returned to Fen's side, hoping his eager joy at spending more time with Fen wasn't plain on his face.

"You need something else?" he asked.

Fen nodded. "Yeah." He turned so his back was to the rest of the helpers in the kitchen, leaning close and sending Char's heart fluttering. "A select group of us are going on a mission. Leaving tomorrow morning, gone overnight, and if all goes well, back the next day. I'm leading with five others in support. It's the first time I'll be gone for more than a day since you started living here, so I wanted to let you know." He paused to study Char's face, and whatever he saw there made him grin. Since Char thought his face was neutral despite the sudden increased thumping of his heart, he had no idea what Fen was seeing. "I didn't want you to worry. Zain is taking temporary commander duties, and Jensen is acting captain for my unit, so go to them if you have any issues."

"I appreciate your letting me know," Char replied, trying to continue his attempt at sounding neutral. Except, his traitorous mouth suddenly added, "Stay safe."

Fen's smile gentled. "I'll be careful. You stay safe too. Don't let the mobs of hungry soldiers trample you." His hand lifted and Char froze in place, wondering what Fen was going to do. His imagination pictured a caress, and Char stomped on that mental image immediately. Fen didn't need to know about the dangerous cliffs Char's traitorous mind kept bringing him to. Fen's hand paused briefly in midair, then went and simply clasped Char on the shoulder. He smiled and nodded, then turned and left.

Jensen remained behind. "Just letting you know; the kid is bunking with Laurence. He gets all the privileges of a full recruit, so three meals a day and laundered clothes, but he's required to put in a full day's work. If he shirks anything, let me know and I'll take him back." He said the last bit loud enough for Karl to hear, and Karl's shoulders hunched in response. "I'll be around at dinner if you have any questions." He left, following after Fen. Char returned to work, hoping reimmersing himself in food would help banish every ridiculous thought Fen's proximity had raised.

Char finished assembling the marinade—oil, red wine, a touch of vinegar, onion and garlic flakes, powdered red pepper for zip, honey, and rosemary—and poured it into large preparation bags. He added the steak rounds, sealed the bags, and put them into the cold box. He kept one bag's worth of marinade in reserve, which he would use to sauté the mushrooms later.

Next, he switched to making dough. He filled his largest bowl with flour, salt, and some sugar, and spent the next few minutes cutting up chunks of cold butter. Once he had enough, he used the large pastry blender to start working the butter into the flour. Getting the butter properly incorporated took a while, and the entire time Char's mind was whirling.

Fen was leaving on an overnight trip, something so specialized that he had to lead the mission personally. That meant it was also dangerous. All Char could do was wish him luck and hope he came back safely, yet that didn't feel at all adequate. There had to be something more Char could do to help ensure Fen's safe return.

His brain flashed to the horrible nightmare of Roe, laughing while she explained how she had poisoned them all, and Char had an idea. He might not be there to rescue Fen if he were captured again, but at least Char could ensure their food was safe to eat. He would need to compromise on dinner preparations, but he thought he might be able to do it.

"I'm done with the beans," Isa called. "What do you need next?"

Char pointed at the large box of apples, the first harvests from the fields. "I need half of those apples peeled, cored and sliced, please."

The dough reached the flaky texture Char liked, so he set aside the pastry blender and went to get cold water. He added the water slowly, mixing it in thoroughly with his hands between each pour, until the dough came together into a firm ball. He wrapped the dough and put it in the cold box, and then moved on to the next task. In another large bowl he mixed cinnamon, sugar, raisins, flour, nutmeg, and zested a lot of lemons.

"What's next for the potatoes?" Ralph suddenly asked, breaking into Char's focus.

Char looked up and saw the pile of peeled potatoes. He set his current lemon down and went to get two massive pots, which he set on the countertop next to Ralph.

"Cut them into chunks about an inch square. They don't need to be exact. Split them evenly between the two pots. Once you're done with that, please peel the garlic and the onions."

Karl was still working on the mushrooms, and it looked like he would be a while longer. Ralph got to work, so Char returned to his lemons. Once he had enough zest, he juiced the denuded lemons, creating a slurry with his spice mixture. He set it aside to wait for the apples.

He paused, and realized he had a few minutes to work on something else. His mind went to his plans for Fen's trip. He was serving pie for dessert tonight, but some chocolate too would go over well. Decided, he pulled out his sheet trays and gave them a light coating with oil. Flour, salt, and baking soda went into one bowl. In a large pot Char measured out butter, sugar, and some water. Once the pot started to boil, he added chopped chocolate and vanilla extract, stirring until the chocolate was completely melted. He transferred the chocolate mixture into a large bowl and set it aside to cool. He went to the cold box and retrieved his dough.

The chilled dough took a lot of effort to roll out, but eventually Char got it to the thickness he wanted. He carefully draped the dough into pie tins, making sure he filled the entire tin before trimming the edges. His original plan had been to do a lattice top, but that took too much time. He would have to reroll the dough and do a full top instead, but for now he wrapped the leftover dough, placed a cloth between each filled tin, and the entire stack went back into the cold box.

Since he was still waiting for the apples, Char checked on his chocolate, sticking a finger into it to gauge the temperature. It had cooled enough. Char cracked eggs in, one at a time, stirring well with his whisk in between each one. Once all the eggs were mixed thoroughly, Char slowly added the flour mixture, making sure not to leave clumps that would dry out when baked. When the flour bowl was finally empty and his arm ached from all the mixing, Char added more chocolate chunks, stirring them in as well. Then he poured the batter into the prepared pans, slotted the pans into the oven, and it was time to return to his pies. The apples were mostly cut. Char went over to help with the last few, letting Isa focus on getting the last handful peeled while Char cored and sliced.

Isa moved on to peeling onions while Char took apples and added them to his cinnamon slurry, coating them thoroughly. He retrieved his dough and evenly distributed the coated apples between all the pie dishes.

He dotted the pies with butter, and then rolled out the remaining dough, which he draped over the pies to form the top crust. He carefully trimmed the edges and pressed the two crusts together with a fork to create a decorative edge. He couldn't help adding some decoration though, using the tip of his paring knife to cut apple shapes in the very center of each crust rather than more mundane slashes for vent holes.

The brownies were done. Char moved them from the oven to a cooling rack and slotted the pies into the oven in their place.

A glance at the clock said he had about fifteen minutes before he had to start on his next task, which was plenty of time to quickly slot in another recipe. Char pulled out flour, salt, and eggs. He dumped the flour into a pile onto a clean countertop, added salt, and gently mixed until the two were incorporated. He made a well in the center of the mound. In a separate bowl Char cracked eggs and used a fork to whisk them together. He poured the eggs into the well, added a bit of cool water, and used the fork to slowly combine the flour and egg—adding more water as needed—until he had a dough. Char set the fork aside and spent the next ten minutes kneading. Once the dough reached the right consistency under his fingers, Char wrapped it and set it aside. When the dinner rush slowed later tonight, he would roll the dough into rounds and use the back of a table knife to turn it into shells. For now, it was time to feed his workers.

"How are the mushrooms?" he asked Karl.

"I'm almost done," Karl said with a heavy, put-upon sigh.

"The potatoes?" Char asked.

Ralph waved his knife in the air briefly. "Also almost done."

"And I'm cleaning the last of the onions," Isa added.

Marcus and Heidi at the sinks glanced over, looking damp and unhappy, likely because the pile of dishes had only grown thanks to Char making pies and brownies. They had chosen dishes over food prep, but they looked like they might be hoping someone would switch off with them.

Mentally calculating for six, Char found a medium-sized pot and filled it with some of the potato chunks. He added water and salt and set the pot onto the stove to boil. He took one of the cleaned onions, sliced it, and set it aside. Next, he took some cleaned mushrooms from Karl and sliced them. By then the potatoes were boiling, so he retrieved six steaks from one of the marinade bags. The steaks went on the grill. The mushrooms went into one olive oil-coated pan with garlic, onion, and a dash of red pepper powder. When the mushrooms had released their water and started reducing, he added a splash of the reserved marinade and covered the pan. The onions went into a second oiled pan, where he let them caramelize. He got another medium pot and filled it halfway with water. He slotted the metal steamer attachment to the top and left it on the stove to start boiling.

He took a fork and tested the potatoes, and when the fork slid right through, he brought that pot over to the sink. He used a pot lid to hold the potatoes inside and drained the water, and then brought the pot over to the counter. He flipped the steaks, then found the masher and squished the potatoes until they were completely mashed. Butter, a dash of milk, and they were smooth and silky. He covered the pot to keep the contents warm and set it aside. The steamer was boiling. He did a five second dice on some dill, then moved the pot to a cooler burner, filled the top with beans, dill, and some butter, and covered it.

"Plates, please," he called. Dishes were dropped into the sink with a splash, onions, mushrooms, and potatoes abandoned, as the entire group rushed over. Char grabbed bowls, putting the onions, mushrooms, and potatoes each in a bowl and slotting serving spoons into them. By then the beans were done, so they went into a fourth bowl with a set of serving tongs.

Everyone received a steak, and then moved down the line of bowls to add the sides. Karl watched for a moment to see what they were doing and then dived in. In Char's experience, street kids, particularly growing ones, were never shy about taking food. Even vegetables, which Karl took without pause. They sat at one of the long tables in the dining area, and for the first few minutes the only noise was the scrape of silverware on plates and chewing.

The steak was still slightly pink in the middle, firm without being rubbery, with pops of flavor from the marinade and the grill. The mushrooms and onions perfectly complemented the steak, especially when mixed with the potato, which Char had kept purposefully bland for that reason. The beans still had some snap but were soft enough to chew, and the dill refreshed the palate between the heaviness of everything else.

All in all, Char was pleased with the meal. Now, all he had to do was cook enough for the hungry residents who would descend on them in about a half hour. He would slice the mushrooms and onions first and get the massive pots of potatoes boiling as well. Fill the grill with steaks, and then he could move over to cutting the brownies. Isa, Ralph, and Karl could plate those, and set up the serving area while Char cooked.

And then he had to find some spare time in all of that to work on his meal preparation for Fen. He already planned to make oatcakes after dinner to serve for breakfast in the morning; making a little extra would be easy enough and that covered breakfast for Fen's group. They would eat lunch in the saddle both days, and Char had plenty of his homemade smoked jerky in storage. That left dinner, which he could make tonight if he stayed up late. Diced onions sautéed in butter, then add flour and milk to make a béchamel. Add cracked black pepper and mustard powder, then wait for it to boil and thicken before adding in his cheeses. Cheddar, Jack, and the Toval mystery-cheese special which was a mass-produced conglomeration of magic-derived uncertainty. It was called Tovalian cheese, although whether it actually had any actual cheese in it was a mystery Char wasn't in a hurry to solve. However, it melted exactly like Char preferred and when combined with the cheddar gave his mac and cheese a smooth creaminess no other cheese could provide. First, though, he would need to form his pasta. The amount of dough he had made would serve about half this facility, but if he made more tomorrow, he could also serve mac and cheese for dinner. He could turn it into a create your own, with various vegetables or meats to add and a couple types of breadcrumbs sautéed for a topping.

First, though, was dinner tonight and Fen's food, and trying not to worry about Fen leaving on a potentially dangerous trip. Trying, but Char knew he would fail.

Chapter Eleven

FOUR IN THE morning was a ridiculous time to be awake. Normally, Char would still be asleep for at least another half hour to forty-five minutes, but needs must and he'd gotten up at three to have a head start. The bag of supplies resting on the table in front of him next to a plate of fresh oatcakes made a half hour ago weighed heavily on Char's mind. Jerky for lunch today and tomorrow, more oatcakes for tomorrow's breakfast, for dinner tonight a pan of mac and cheese under a protective lid with instructions for heating if Fen could have a fire, but which could also be eaten cold, and a double portion of brownies. All Char needed was Fen to appear so he could pass over the bundle.

Finally, Char heard footsteps down the hallway and a few seconds later Fen walked into the common area.

"Char?" he asked, catching sight of Char almost immediately. "What are you doing here?"

"I made some food for your trip," Char explained, pointing to the bag.

Fen's eyes lit up and he smiled. "That's amazing. Thanks so much!"

He walked over and sat on the couch next to Char, close enough their knees touched. Char blinked, suddenly way too close to Fen's disarming hazel eyes. Fen reached out with one hand, and this time he didn't hesitate, trailing his fingers along Char's cheek and tucking a strand of hair behind Char's ear in a gentle caress that sent fire shooting through Char's entire body.

"I really am glad I didn't kill you," Fen said, his voice low and growly. His fingers trailed behind Char's ear and down his jaw until Fen pulled away when he reached Char's chin.

Char's brain had turned to pudding; the chocolate kind, redolent in vanilla bean and utterly sinful. Still, a small part of him was engaged enough to wonder how long Fen had been using that phrase in place of saying, "I love you."

Char opened his mouth to respond and only air came out, breathy and almost a sigh, and his face went hot. Fen smiled, his eyes burning as he looked at Char, catching all of the minutia of Char's reaction.

He suddenly pulled away to a polite distance. Char's brain took a second to reengage and recognize the sound of footsteps in the hallway. The rest of Fen's group emerged and joined them at the couches.

"Char made us food for the trip," Fen explained, picking up the bag.

"Yes!" Laurence cheered, although quietly so he didn't wake the rest of the building.

"And oatcakes for this morning," Char added. He held out the plate, which was empty a half second later.

"You're the best," Naomi said through a full mouth.

"It's the least I can do to help you have a safe trip," Char explained. "I expect to see everyone for dinner tomorrow night." He said the last bit to the group, but his eyes were focused on Fen.

Fen nodded. "We'll be there. I promise." His gaze was locked with Char's for a long moment before he wrenched himself away. "Let's go. Daylight's wasting," he said to his group, leading the way outside into the scant predawn light just starting to glow on the eastern horizon.

The door closed behind the last of them with a thud, and Char sank back into the couch cushion, letting out a heavy sigh.

Fen loved him? No, that wasn't possible, and yet that caress and the meaning behind those words said otherwise. Fen wasn't someone to dally or to arrange conquests; no, if he was expressing interest in Char that way, it was because he meant it. Maybe Char was misinterpreting. He could be projecting his own inner wishes over Fen's words. Yet Fen was the one to reach out and touch Char, the one to say those specific words in that deep tone, and Char was utterly confused.

He would have to wait until Fen returned to figure out what was real and what part was his brain going off into a lovely fantasy, but perhaps for the next two days Char could dream.

And in the meantime, he had breakfast to prepare. Char stood and headed back toward the kitchen. The bread and rolls he had made yesterday and left overnight to rise needed to go in the oven. In addition to the oatcakes, today was scrambled eggs as well; two different kinds to please multiple palates. The first completely plain, only eggs scrambled in butter. On the side he would offer bowls of shredded cheese, salt and pepper, and his homemade salsa. To the second version, he would add milk, salt, and pepper to the eggs before cooking, and directly after he put the eggs in the pan, he would add cheese. Cooked low and slow, the cheese melted and incorporated into the egg, making for a creamier and fluffier final product. Particularly when Char used Tovalian cheese, although he liked Swiss or Jack as well.

And any free moments he had, Char would be rolling pasta shells off the end of a table knife, trying to make enough to feed the entire complex mac and cheese for dinner that night.

Char walked into his kitchen and let out a breath. With food and cooking to distract him, he might make it through the next two days with his sanity intact. He hoped.

The five o'clock wake-up bell rang from the nearby tower, and the building began to hum with activity as everyone not on night shifts began their day. Char's morning crew arrived not long after. Two volunteered to start washing the pile of dirty dishes, and Char directed the other two to the large chunks of cheese and the handheld shredders. Then Karl walked in.

He didn't look awake or happy, but he was on time. Char had to give him a decent grade for effort. That was, until Char took a closer look. Dots of last night's marinade spotted Karl's white shirt and Karl's hair was greasy from not being washed. Char stopped cracking eggs into a bowl, rinsed his hands, and went over to Karl.

"Let's have a chat about my expectations for you working here," Char said, leading Karl over to a table to sit. "Good hygiene is the most important thing you or I can bring to a kitchen. I expect you to shower at least once every day, scrubbing head to toe with soap. Every morning you will wear clean clothes, and if you spill on yourself during the day, you will go change." Karl opened his mouth, no doubt to protest since he had started scowling at Char's first words, but Char spoke over him. "If you want to continue working in my kitchen, you will obey these simple rules. Now, go shower and come back when you're ready to get to work."

Karl left. Slouching and grimacing, but he went. Char returned to his eggs.

The first rush hit exactly at 6:00 a.m. when the doors opened, and Char worked flat out on making more eggs as the large serving bowls kept emptying. When that rush died down, Char knew they had about a half hour before the second rush hit, mostly comprised of the fifty or so servants who completed morning chores first and ate after.

"Hey, break time. Let's eat while we have a chance," Char called to his four helpers. Karl had yet to reappear, and if he didn't show up by the time they were done eating, Char would have to send Omir out hunting for him. Omir would appreciate the break from shredding yet more cheese.

Char let his helpers line up ahead of him, watching them fill their plates and grab cups of tea. Char was just reaching for a plate when someone walked into the dining hall. He was trained to let customers enjoy before he did, so Char stepped back and turned to look, words of welcome on the tip of his tongue.

The man wasn't wearing the usual brown pants and white shirt of the rest of the royal guard, nor was he wearing armor that said he was going on or off duty. In fact, Char didn't recognize him at all, and Char was getting pretty good with at least knowing the faces of all his regular customers. The man's clothes didn't look like anything from any of the other military units in the complex either, what with the embroidery at the hems and cuffs and the tailored, personalized cut of the jacket.

The man looked around for a minute, caught sight of Char, and walked over, his stride arrogant and full of purpose.

"I've heard this is the best place to eat around here," he said, his lip curling slightly into a full-on sneer.

If all he wanted was some food, Char was happy to feed him, but Char had a sinking feeling he really wanted something else. Still, Char could play along.

When Char had first started cooking here about a month ago during his trial and error—mostly error—period, word had gotten out to other units within the military complex that his food was much better than any of the other dining halls. There had been a sudden influx of additional people to feed, none of whom Char had planned or budgeted for. He had trouble keeping the serving area full of food, and often ran out of ingredients before the meal times ended. Fen had stepped in and brought over a wide-mouthed jar, which lived on the end of the serving counter closest to the door.

"Visitors are always welcome," Char replied. "However, anyone who doesn't have the commander's permission is required to give a donation first." He waved toward the jar. Since most soldiers weren't paid nearly enough, the crowds of outsiders had immediately vanished. Food was free for them in the other halls after all. Occasionally, some soldiers from other units still stopped by to "treat themselves," as they referred to it, but the numbers were much more manageable now.

The man sneered at the jar. He moved closer to Char and bent his head as if he wanted to share a secret. "Someone with your talents deserves a much nicer kitchen than this. If you're willing to work with me, I can ensure you move up in culinary society."

Karl walked in the door. His hair was still damp, and his cheeks red from scrubbing or the hot water, but he was clean. He saw the stranger and froze, going wide-eyed in shocked recognition. Apparently, Karl knew who the man was, even when only able to look at the man's back.

Char took a step farther away from the stranger and said, with his eyes focused on Karl pointedly, "Sir, I'm sure Vice-Captain Jensen would be happy to hear about your ideas."

Karl nodded, spun, and dashed back out the door.

The man frowned at Char. "You're going to miss out on a rare opportunity if you say no to me," he said, his voice still low and cajoling, although notes of anger had crept in.

Char took another step backward. "I like working here, and I don't have any need for help getting anywhere in society." Char was aware his four helpers as well as the few stragglers still at the tables had all abandoned their plates and were coming over, at which point this would get uglier than it already was. Luckily, Jensen strode into the room before it reached that point.

Jensen didn't look winded or as if he had been dragged here from some other task, but Karl dashed in behind him, and he was panting for breath.

"Second Minister Protus, what brings you here?" Jensen asked, walking swiftly over to Protus's side. "I wasn't aware the royal guard had an inspection today. Is this a surprise one?" He grinned widely at Protus. "Come, we can talk in Commander Fenwick's office." He waved one hand in the direction of the doors, still smiling. Protus huffed but went, and Char let out a heavy breath of relief as Protus vanished from view.

"Thank you," Char said to Karl.

"Luckily the captain was in his office, just at the top of the stairs," Karl explained. "But, man, he's fast. The second I said you were in trouble, poof! Now I know why I failed their running test thing."

"Nah," Omir cut in, clapping Karl genially on the back. "Jensen's just really fast. No one can beat him on the track. You failed because you're slow and out of shape." He eyed Karl's skinny frame with a wry twist to his lips that said he had also noticed how underfed Karl looked. "Anyway, time's a'wastin. Better get your breakfast before the mobs reappear."

Karl didn't wait to be told twice, grabbing a plate and filling it. Char followed, and joined the rest of his morning crew as everyone took their seats at a nearby table.

"You recognized Protus?" Char asked Karl, who was busy stuffing his face.

Karl nodded. "He's in charge of the court stuff for the military," he replied, his mouth full. To everyone's relief, he swallowed before continuing. "Minimum sentence for a first offense of attempted robbery is a month. He sentenced me to six. Of course I'm gonna remember someone that nasty."

"I wonder what he was doing here, then?" Sherri asked. She reached out and repositioned Karl's hand around his fork—reminding Char that she had kids of her own—so he wasn't holding it like a shovel.

"I'm sure Jensen is finding that out right now," Char answered. He had emptied his plate, and he needed to get back into the kitchen to start prepping lunch and to continue rolling pasta for dinner, but he had been up since three and taking the respite to enjoy being off his feet was far too tempting.

He definitely found it interesting Protus had approached him the first morning Fen was away. He also wondered if someone else in the room had been closely watching Char's response to report back. Char completely understood the position he was in. His life might revolve almost exclusively around food and cooking, but Char wasn't completely checked out of reality. He was an outsider of origins that hadn't been made public, with access to a royal prince and the entirety of the royal guard. And, if anyone had seen how close Fen and Char had been sitting this morning—had seen Fen's caress of Char's face or the way Char had melted like butter in a hot pan—they would know Char was even closer to Fen than just being his private chef.

"Don't worry," Omir said. "A whole bunch of people saw him try to threaten you today. No one gossips as much as soldiers. Give it an hour and every royal guard will know what happened, and I bet an honor guard will be in place by tonight. By tomorrow every soldier in this complex will know too, and they'll add to your protection detail. No one threatens one of our own." He grinned at Char.

"Thanks," Char replied with a smile in return.

The first diners of the morning's second rush began trickling in. Char sighed but started collecting his dishes.

"Time to get back to work."

Chapter Twelve

CHAR OPENED HIS eyes and let out a breath. Even after a bad night's sleep, he was still conditioned to get up at 4:30 every morning. The first forlorn chirps of birdsong were starting to ring out as a faint line of light colored the horizon. Sunrise was getting later and later as autumn really set in. It was time to start thinking about canning and bottling supplies for winter to supplement the jams and various sauces Char had already added into storage. Even if the city imported hothouse fruits and vegetables, they would be more expensive, and Char had a budget to adhere to. Everything he could bottle now would save him a ton later.

That was where he ought to be focused, yet somehow swirling thoughts and worries about Fen intruded into his plans to buy enough vinegar to start pickling. Those worries had kept him tossing and turning all night, wondering how Fen's mission was going, whether they were safe, and whether they had been able to cook the mac and cheese or been forced to eat it cold. Had the discovery of the brownies at the bottom of the bag buoyed their spirits?

Char groaned and rubbed his hands down his face. Resolute, he threw his blankets back and climbed out of bed, heading to the wardrobe where his work clothes hung.

His room had slowly changed over the last three months. The second bed and two armor and weapons stands had vanished within a day, but eventually the two dressers and one of the blanket trunks had gone as well. His bed was turned ninety degrees and the headboard pushed against a side wall, opposite of which one longer dresser had been placed. A nightstand stood on the window side of the bed, and under the window was the remaining blanket trunk. Char quite liked the setup and as soon as he figured out which servant was responsible, he would definitely thank them. He also appreciated someone—probably Fen—had decided he got to have his own room.

Char finished getting dressed and headed down to the bathroom to wash his face. A few minutes later, he arrived into the familiar comfort of his kitchen. He tied an apron around his waist and fired up the ovens, before going to check his bread and rolls. They had risen perfectly overnight and were ready to bake once the ovens were hot enough. In the meantime, he was thinking pancakes for breakfast: one plain, and the other made with fresh blueberries inside. He needed flour and a bunch of ingredients from the pantry. Char pulled open the door to the deep room with floor to ceiling shelving on all three walls, then froze.

Something wasn't right.

The bag of apples was open, Char noticed immediately. He kept everything in the pantry sealed to prevent bugs or animals. Some of the jars on one of the lower shelves had been moved as if someone had picked them up to try to open them. Char gingerly checked them, but his magic had been used to vacuum seal them and whomever or whatever had tried to open them didn't have the strength to pop the lid.

Visions of Roe dosing the food with poison danced through Char's mind as he walked deeper into the pantry. Except, the situation was far odder than that. Only things on the lowest shelf or the floor had been touched, aside from where the bag of potatoes had been knocked over and the two indentations in the bag revealed how the jars on the second shelf directly above had been reached.

Any non-perishable leftovers were moved to the common areas when the kitchen closed at night, so there was plenty of food available for anyone coming in from a late shift or who wanted a midnight snack. They also knew better than to touch Char's stores, something Fen had made very clear early on after some innocent late-night foraging attempts had disrupted some of Char's meal planning. Which meant either something sinister had occurred, or something very strange.

Char spun around and stomped out of the pantry, intent on checking the cold box, and stuttered to another shocked freeze. Someone was leaning on the counter, waiting for him.

The helpers assigned to morning duty—and Karl—wouldn't arrive for another half hour; they were probably still asleep. Besides, the stranger was dressed head to toe in black and standing in the shadowed area since Char hadn't bothered to light any of the mage lights outside of his prep area.

"The kitchen doesn't open until six," Char said, trying to make out any of the stranger's features. All he saw was shadow and dark.

"My master has an offer for you, one you can't afford to refuse," the stranger said. The voice was airy and higher pitched, yet masculine at the same time. Char couldn't distinguish a gender by the sound.

"I refuse," Char responded immediately, uninterested in what this scary individual had to offer. If it were something aboveboard, they would have met with Char when there was an audience, not at a quarter to five in the morning, and certainly not with any distinguishing features concealed. And also not when Fen was conveniently away.

"My master can give you riches beyond all belief. You would never have to work another day in your life; never have to slave in another kitchen again," the stranger added, their voice cajoling.

Char rolled his eyes. "Your master didn't do his homework if he thought that would tempt me," he replied, scoffing. Telling Char he'd never need to work in a kitchen again was guaranteed to make him say no. "Go tell him to take his scheming elsewhere. I have pancakes to make."

"I will leave you to think over my master's offer," the stranger said, as if they hadn't heard Char's answer. "If you decline further, my master's next offer will not be as friendly."

The stranger turned and walked away, deeper into the darkened area of the room and then through the glass double doors leading into the massive courtyard outside. With only dimming stars to light the way, Char quickly lost sight of them.

Char let out a slow breath and rubbed his sweaty palms against his hips to dry them. That was now two people who had offered him things for no apparent reason. At least they had caught the first, but this second one seemed a touch more dangerous. Plus, someone had been rummaging through his pantry, Char remembered. The stranger was long gone; running to get Jensen now would only wake Jensen early for no reason and delay breakfast preparations. Char would catch Jensen when he came in for food.

What Char could do right now was check the cold box to see if his suspicions might be correct, so when he told Jensen about the food-stealing visitor he could provide some evidence. Char popped open the door to the cold box and wasn't surprised to see the cheese on the lower shelf had been moved around, and the smaller brick of cheddar was completely gone. Nothing on any of the higher shelves appeared to have been touched.

Definitely curious, but Char didn't think anything nefarious had occurred. Unfortunately, there wasn't anything he could do about it now, and dwelling on it wouldn't get his bread cooked. Char pulled out the last of yesterday's milk and closed the door. He left the milk on the counter and went to his bread, which had risen on trays set into his tall cooling rack. The larger loaves took longer to cook, so Char filled his ovens with those first, checking the clock and setting a mental timer.

He retrieved the rest of his ingredients to make pancake batter and got to work, mixing the dry ingredients in one bowl and the wet in a second, so he would be ready to combine the two when it came time to cook. Char had two secret touches he used when making pancakes that made them extra fluffy. The main one was he included bananas, about one banana for four servings and the darker the outer skin the better—depending on the size of the banana, of course. He used a fork to squish the bananas into a chunky paste to mix into the flour with the wet ingredients. His second trick was to never use a spoon to mix the batter. He only used a fork and his arm strength, since a whisk couldn't handle how thick the batter got, and this added air and volume to the batter even before it was cooked.

And all the while, Char kept looking around, glancing over his shoulder and half expecting yet another visitor to appear. When the doors opened to admit the morning's helpers, Char let out a breath. At least now if he did get a visit from another unwelcome stranger, he had backup.

Char removed the bread from the oven, setting it aside on racks to cool, then put in the rolls while he waited for his helpers to find their aprons and conduct a few rounds of rock/paper/scissors to decide which two got stuck with the dishwashing.

He set the two soldiers who didn't get sink duty to cleaning fruit, particularly the blueberries for the pancakes, but also strawberries, cantaloupe, honeydew, kiwi, and raspberries for a fruit salad. Blueberries were a spring fruit, and not something Char was likely to get his hands on for a few months, so he had them wash every carton still in the fridge. After the breakfast rush ended, Char would start making jam and pie filling, both of which he would bottle to use over winter. He wished he could dry blueberries too, but there weren't enough hours in the day for that. Maybe he would be able to buy some the next time he went to market.

At some point he would have to start bottling the summer and autumn fruits too—the strawberries, raspberries, and blackberries—but one set of fruits at a time.

"What do you want me to do?" Karl asked.

Char grinned at him and passed him a fork. "You see all those bruised bananas?" Char asked, pointing to the open pantry door and the three bunches of blackening bananas on the third shelf to the left. "I need you to peel and mash them until they look like this," Char explained, showing Karl the contents of one of the large bowls he had been working with. "I need thirty added to this bowl, and another thirty into another bowl."

Char's pancakes were in good shape, timewise. He had one massive bowl of dry ingredients, a second of the wet, and only the third, with the bananas, wasn't actually ready. Pancakes were much better served fresh off the griddle, so Char left Karl to prepare the last part and moved on to his next recipe.

Besides, now that the complex was awake, Char didn't have to feel guilty about making noise.

Karl didn't have any trouble reaching the bananas three shelves high, as Char suspected, and once he was done in the pantry Char retrieved his bag of shelled walnuts. Shelled cost extra but saved so much time it was worth the expense. He measured out what he wanted and put them in a separate bag, then took out his metal mallet and started slamming it into the nuts in a *bang bang bang* that would definitely be audible in the bedrooms. Once the nuts were in tiny pieces, he set them aside.

Batter for muffins was incredibly easy. Once it was ready, he split it into two separate bowls. First, he commandeered a large portion of the washed and dried raspberries, chopping them smaller and mixing those into one bowl. He removed the rolls from the oven and replaced them with the first batches of raspberry muffins. He moved on to the banana walnut next, as Karl made progress with peeling and squishing bananas, mixing in the nuts and bananas to the other half of the batter.

By the time the last batch of muffins was in the ovens, he was ready to start cooking pancakes. Char did take a few minutes to cube the melons—wishing he had a sous chef he trusted to cut near-identical sized squares—and then focused on heating up the griddle and oiling it. Karl finished with the bananas, and then he and the other two helpers went out to start setting up the room, turning on lights and plattering cooled bread for the serving area. Char mixed the three bowls of ingredients together with his fork, happy with the resulting pancake batter, then started pouring circles onto the griddle.

The morning passed quickly. Char was busy studying the bubbles forming in the cooking pancakes to ensure he flipped them at just the right moment, but every time a new group of diners entered the room, he glanced up to see if Jensen was with them.

As the initial rush began to abate, Jensen finally strode into the room. However, rather than grabbing a plate, he headed to the side of the kitchen and waved Char over. Char slid a spatula underneath the cooking pancakes, gauging whether the bottoms were as toasty brown as the tops. They were, so he quickly transferred them over to a platter, which one of his helpers whisked away to replace the nearly empty one in the serving area. Char turned the heat down on the griddle, wiped his hands on his apron, and headed over, hopeful Jensen would be able to help him solve the mysteries of both his visitors.

Chapter Thirteen

"I'VE GOTTEN WORD from Fen," Jensen said, his voice low so it wouldn't carry. He had turned his back to the rest of the room so no one could read his lips either. "His mission was successful, so he'll be back tonight." Char grinned, very happy to hear that, but then Jensen continued. "Fen…er. He wanted me to tell you they were able to heat the mac and cheese last night and it was delicious. Used an entire line in the missive, too," he added, grumbling.

"He was able to heat it!" Char breathed out, ecstatic. Fen was returning safely and he had liked Char's food!

Jensen abruptly stopped grumbling, looking at Char sharply for a moment before letting out a sigh.

"Anyway," he continued. "I expect him to be back in time for dinner. Don't do anything special, since we're supposed to pretend he was never away on a secret mission."

"Right," Char replied.

His dinner plans were for semi-deconstructed chicken pot pies, which were normal enough. Start with a roux on the stove. Add in milk and spices, particularly a lot of sage. Then shred chicken breast poached in stock from one of Char's bouillon cubes. Add in partially cooked vegetables and stir together. Pour all that into massive baking dishes and dot the top with chunks of uncooked biscuit dough. Once baked, the biscuits expanded to create the illusion of individual portions.

"I was thinking of making chocolate cakes anyway. Since my cold box is currently stuffed full with raspberries, I'll do a raspberry coulis. Nothing too fancy, and as long as we only tell Fen and his group they're celebration cakes, no one will ever know."

"Sounds delicious to me," Jensen replied, swallowing saliva reflexively. "I'll make sure to tell Fen you made the cakes for him."

"Thanks. And thanks for letting me know he's coming back soon." Char took a deep breath and let it out. "I had two visitors this morning," he said when Jensen looked at him curiously. Jensen immediately scowled.

"Who?" he snapped, somehow managing to keep his voice low even as anger threaded through it.

Char shook his head. "I have no idea. I noticed some food had been moved around in the pantry and was heading over to check the cold box when a person offered me rather a lot of money to agree to work for their master."

"Wait. Someone moved around food in your pantry and then tried to hire you?" Jensen asked, his quizzical expression saying he was trying to figure out what Char was explaining.

"I think I had two separate visitors," Char said, trying to explain clearer a second time. "The first was sometime overnight. They were only tall enough to reach the lowest shelves in the pantry and the cold box. I was wondering if children are allowed in the complex."

"Generally no. There is a small section on the exact opposite side of the complex from here where high-level leaders can choose to live in houses with their immediate families, and a school and such to serve for any children. But you've got to be at Fen's level—a commander—or higher to be eligible. The kids generally stay around there, although occasionally one will get lost and wander around. Never heard of one pilfering food before. What about the person who offered you money? Can you describe them?"

"No." Char shook his head. "They purposefully stood in the shadows, and it was before five this morning, so the sun hadn't risen yet. They were wearing all black and might have had something covering their face too, but I couldn't tell."

"And they offered you money?"

"'Riches beyond belief' were the words they used. Said I'd never have to work another day in my life or step into a kitchen again." Char scowled, running his hands down his apron in proprietary pride.

Jensen snorted out a laugh. "Offering you a new kitchen would have been more effective."

Char sighed pointedly in exasperation, although he did offer a grin for the joke. "After I refused, they said they would return for my answer, and if it wasn't what they wanted to hear threats would be next."

Jensen was quiet for a few long moments, frowning as he presumably mulled over Char's words.

"I'm assigning you a bodyguard," he said finally. "Someone who isn't distracted by washing dishes or food prep, one whose only job is to make certain you're safe. That should help with the unwelcome visitors threatening you until your newness and connection to Fen has time to blow over. I'm not certain what to do about the food thief though."

"Tell me about Karl," Char requested first, trying to get as much fact to support his supposition before telling Jensen his idea.

"If Karl had stolen food, he would have taken from higher shelves," Jensen replied immediately.

"Agreed. I'm wondering about his home situation before he was taken in by the courts."

Jensen frowned at Char again but answered readily enough. "He was a street kid, as far as I'm aware. No home life to speak of."

"Everything I've ever heard about street kids indicates they struggle to survive alone. I've seen the news articles about street gangs, or the so-called thieves guild..."

Jensen was already shaking his head as Char trailed off. "He was checked for any tattoos or any of the sashes or other clothing worn by those group members, and there weren't any signs he was a member of a larger group. Besides, even if one of the gang members targets the military, they're always sent to regular court instead. Only the unaffiliated ones go to a military tribunal. Karl's not part of anything like that, but you're probably correct that he was part of some kind of group, just to survive. I can look into it if you think that might be helpful."

Char shrugged. "I'm wondering if any of his group members followed him here, perhaps someone small enough they can only reach the bottom shelves."

Jensen's eyebrow lifted in surprise, and then he grinned. "That would be something if they could sneak past the guarded gate of the military complex and are hiding somewhere inside the barracks for the elite royal guard. That would be someone I'd want to hire." He grinned. "It sounds like you might have an idea of how to catch them?"

"Not really. I was thinking they know this is a poorly guarded room at night with easy access to food, and no alarm was raised this morning after last night's theft. I figure they'll come back tonight, and I'd hang around until they showed up."

Jensen thought about Char's plan for a few moments before he nodded once sharply. "Right. I'll have your bodyguard assigned by then, and I'll brief them on the situation ahead of time. After you catch the thief, come upstairs to Fen's office so we can figure out how to deal with the problem."

"Will do," Char replied.

Jensen clapped Char on the shoulder and went to go fill a plate. Char returned to the griddle, where he would turn out another platter of pancakes before starting lunch preparations, which required making a massive batch of mayonnaise for the tuna, salmon, chicken, and ham salads he was going to offer in a make-your-own sandwich bar.

The rest of the day passed quickly; Char too focused on making food to worry about anything else. He taught Karl how to make the mayo, giving him a tutorial on whisking eggs, which he seemed to enjoy, and then moved into the frenzy of keeping fresh trays of pot pie cooked and ready as the rush of hungry diners descended for dinner.

And then Fen walked into the room.

He looked completely normal, as if he hadn't been anywhere in particular the past thirty-six hours. Dressed in the same white shirt and brown pants as everyone else, he would have blended in completely had Char not had some sort of sixth sense for when Fen was around. Something under Char's breastbone relaxed at the sight, and Char smiled to himself even as he continued placing rounded chunks of raw biscuit dough onto the next pan of pot pie to go into the oven.

Fen went to the end of the serving line and picked up a plate. Char tried not to watch him too obviously, sneaking glances to check whether he had any bruising or a residual limp to indicate he had recently been healed.

Char removed a cooked pot pie tray from the oven, slotting the new one in its place, and let his crew haul the food out to the serving area. When he looked up again, Fen was standing across from him, the width of the serving area and stovetop all that separated them. Fen opened his mouth to say something, but then Zain's voice echoed through the room.

"Hey, Fen, get your ass over here!" she yelled from the table on the other side of the room, where she sat with Jensen and a couple of the other leaders.

Fen closed his mouth on a grimace and let out a sigh, before mouthing, "Talk to you later." He finished filling his plate and left, Char trying hard not to watch him walk through the crowded tables.

Char forced his attention back to his big pot, which had been delivered freshly cleaned and dried. He made a quick roux, added milk and chicken stock and waited for it to thicken and boil, before tossing in all the already cooked vegetables and chicken. He added spices, waited for the concoction to return to a boil and thicken properly, and then poured it out into another massive baking dish. He moved over to a counter to start dotting it with biscuit dough. By the time the new dish was ready, the cooking one was complete, so he swapped them. The rest of the evening continued in the same endless cycle, the pot pie vanishing alarmingly fast as diners returned to the serving area for seconds or even thirds.

Finally, the rush died down. Char slotted another pie into the oven, and when he stood, he took a moment to stretch his back. At this point of the evening, Karl and three of his four helpers were busy washing dishes while the fourth maintained the serving area and bussed the dish return station.

"Let's take a break and have dinner," Char called to them. He didn't need to repeat himself as all five immediately stopped what they were doing and headed to fill their plates. Char followed them.

The beauty of pot pie was it was an entire meal in one bite. Vegetables, protein, and starch—everything hungry soldiers needed to refuel after a busy day—were all encompassed within the bake itself. The side salad Char had also served was almost untouched. That was okay, since the lettuce was fresh enough, so he could serve it again for lunch tomorrow. The chocolate cakes were almost gone, another dish for which people had gone back for more. He cut himself a small slice and added it to his plate next to the pot pie and then joined his crew at a table to eat.

Sage, garlic, onion, hearty cream, redolent chicken stock. Different textures between the springy chicken, soft potato, and gentle snap of the vegetables. The crunch of the biscuit, plus the buttery bread cutting through the heavy roux. Perfection in a pot pie. Char closed his eyes as he chewed, letting all the flavors meld across his tongue.

He hadn't enjoyed the previous evening's mac and cheese nearly as much, which was strange because he actually usually liked that dish better. The knot under his breastbone had unraveled at the sight of Fen, which made the pungent sage far more enjoyable in comparison to last night's sharp bite of cheddar. Of course, at some point Char would have to decide what to do about his feelings and whether Fen actually returned them. That thought almost soured his taste buds, but the raspberry coulis in the cake was already sour, so Char didn't notice too much.

"One of these days I'm going to figure it out," Naomi said, sighing heavily. The front of her apron was soaked, little bubbles still popping in the seams, from her stint at dishwashing.

"Figure what out?" Karl asked, his cheeks puffed out with biscuit, spraying crumbs.

"Hey!" Steve growled, raising a hand to shield his food. "Don't talk with your mouth full, kid!"

"How Char goes from raw carrots and hard-ass potatoes to this," Naomi replied, waving her hand over the remnants of pot pie on her plate and blithely ignoring Karl and Steve beginning to squabble. "If I was this good at cooking, my husband would be working in the military, and I'd be home with our kids. Luckily, he's got a decent hand at keeping everyone fed and happy, because I sure don't." She sighed again.

"I don't mind teaching you, although the best teacher is actually the doing, so everyone who's been helping with cleaning and preparing the food is learning how to do it for themselves someday."

Naomi laughed. "I volunteer for dish duty for a reason. You don't want me anywhere near anything potentially edible until it's on my own plate and halfway into my mouth. I promise you."

"Which is why our Commander Fen went to his dad, the king, and practically begged for the money to reopen this kitchen," Arnold added. He tapped his nose. "Or so the rumors say, at least. I don't think any of the staff at the communal kitchen know what they're doing either, let alone any of us. I think we were all desperate for a good meal, commander included."

Char ducked his head, hoping they wouldn't notice his blush despite the heat radiating from his cheeks. Fen had done that for him? Char could believe it, considering the way Fen had smiled when he saw Char in the courtyard outside the palace. Also considering their conversation before Fen had left on his mission. But Char wasn't thinking about that right now. Since he was done eating and the dinner rush had passed, he ought to be plotting how to catch the food thief.

They cleared their plates and returned to work. Char removed his last dish of pot pie from the oven and turned it off. They wouldn't need to make any more tonight. His helpers focused on washing dishes as the last few stragglers came in to eat. Char turned his focus to making bread dough to rise overnight, mixing his flour, salt, sugar, oil, and yeast from one of his starters he kept in the fridge. For the brioche, he added milk and butter without the oil, mixing until he had a dough formed, then started to knead. Karl wandered over from the sink, his apron and shirt plastered to his chest with water, and stood nearby to watch as Char pressed out the dough, turned it, and pressed again, forming the elasticity needed for the bread to rise properly in the oven. He made three separate batches, which he put into three different bowls. He set those aside to rise. The rolls were a very similar recipe with milk and butter but omitted eggs.

"Are your hands dry?" Char asked Karl when he was done kneading the last batch. By then, the first batch had risen for long enough.

Karl held out his hands and nodded. "Yeah. Why?"

Char pulled over the round pans he used to bake the rolls. "Take a chunk of dough about this size," Char explained, showing Karl. "move it gently between your palms, like this, until it forms a ball. Then place it in the pan, nicely spread out so they have room to grow."

He left Karl to it, keeping half an eye on him, but moved on to cinnamon roll dough next as the main component for the morning's breakfast.

The dough itself was similar to the rest, just with different proportions of everything. He made six triple batches, hoping that would be enough, and set the dough aside for the first rise.

By then the brioche was done rising. Char slotted the bowls into the cold box and marked them with the tag so the servants who started mopping at four in the morning knew to take them out and put them onto the counters or racks to give the bread time to come to room temperature before Char baked them in the morning.

He made his cinnamon sugar recipe next, at which point the cinnamon roll dough had rested enough. He rolled out the first batch until it reached the correct thickness, then dotted it liberally with butter and coated it with cinnamon sugar. He rolled it up into a log and cut the log into slices using some sewing thread. A knife would squish the dough, making them oblong rather than round. He placed them in a baking dish, covered it, slotted it into the cold box, tagged it, and then returned to roll out more dough.

This might be mindless, fairly monotonous work, but he enjoyed the slowdown at the end of the day, without the rush and bustle. Arnold came over to wipe down the countertops when Char took the last batch to the cold box, Karl following behind with his rolls. They had to dodge around Naomi and Stan, who were fitting the leftovers into the cold box as well. Sheryl was turning off the lights in the dining area. Pretty soon the kitchen was dim and quiet, as if all the appliances were children settled under the covers in bed, drifting off into dreamland.

Speaking of children and bedtimes... "Karl, head on to bed," Char called.

Karl's immediate scowl was cut off by a wide yawn. He scuffed his feet a few times on the way, but he went. The rest of Char's helpers headed off to their own evening activities soon after. Char made himself a cup of tea—plain chamomile for this time of night—turned off the rest of the lights, and settled into a chair at one of the tables where he was out of the direct line of sight from the doors.

Only twenty minutes later, the set of double doors leading to the dorm where Char lived slid open. Char tensed, freezing in place and straining his ears in the dark for the slightest sound. A moment later, Fen stepped into a beam of moonlight shining through the courtyard windows.

Chapter Fourteen

CHAR FROZE IN place and sucked in a shocked breath, feeling a bit like a bunny staring down the throat of a hungry wolf. Yet at the same time, this was Fen and Char wasn't frightened; he just didn't know how to react or what to say.

Fen looked around for a few moments, squinting in the dark, but when he finally caught sight of Char a happy smile broke out, brightening his eyes as they reflected the moonlight.

"I heard you were having some difficulty with unwanted visitors," he said, his voice soft so it didn't echo in the empty room and alert Char's prey that he was lying in wait. Fen walked over and took the seat across the table from Char, the length of wood between them a welcome shield of separation. "I volunteered to be your guard this evening," he added, his smile still bright and happy.

Char struggled with what he wanted to say, but emotion beat out logic in the words that popped out. "You have to be exhausted. You've barely been back after your trip!"

Fen stifled a laugh behind one hand, his grin widening. The way his eyes twinkled said he thought Char was being cute, which wasn't Char's intention.

"That's why I don't have stacks of paperwork with me right now," Fen explained. "Or any aides circling me like hungry sharks, demanding I sign things. I'm going to relax here with you, have a pleasant chat, and hopefully take ten minutes to subdue whoever might show up. Jensen can handle logistics for one more night," he added with a wink.

Char ducked his head, blushing again. Fen reached across the table, his fingertips brushing under Char's chin, as he gently lifted Char's head. He kept the contact even as their eyes caught, trailing his touch along Char's jaw and up to his cheek before slowly pulling back. Char couldn't blink; couldn't look away. Staring into Fen's hazel eyes, the warmth and welcoming drew Char in until his body started to lean forward, crossing the short distance of a few feet of wood. Fen met him halfway, their lips touching in a gentle busk at first and then more firmly.

An initial blast slammed into Char, like biting into a chili and the heady thrill of drinking straight brandy combined with the sweet anticipation that arose the moment before a spoon cracked through the hard sugar coating of a crème brûlée followed by the ease of delicate savory custard. Char didn't know when his eyes slid closed, but he tilted his head, wanting more. Closer. To feel and taste and wonder.

Char let out an involuntary mewl when Fen pulled away. Fen gave a sheepish shrug, his cheeks flushed and his eyes burning, and he pointed at the doors leading into their barracks. One of them was popped open a bare inch, as if someone was on the other side, listening for any noise in the kitchen. Char froze in place, suppressing his panting breaths, and then slowly eased himself back into his seat.

The door slid open another inch, and then a bit farther, until it was wide enough for someone small to scuttle through. In the darkness, all Char could make out was a slim form a little over three feet tall making a beeline to the pantry. Char waited for the child to get inside the shelved space before he got up and walked into the kitchen. He flicked the switch to turn on the mage lights, and the child let out a shocked squeal.

The little girl was maybe six years old. She stood in the middle of the pantry, her eyes wide with surprise as they darted between Char and Fen. She was already holding a green apple in one hand, the other outstretched and frozen, about to grab a second. Her hair was brown and her eyes a familiar golden brown—the same exact shade as Karl's. One of the regulation white shirts hung off her shoulders like an oversized dress, belted at the waist with a length of tatty rope.

"How are you related to Karl?" Char asked, keeping his voice gentle and polite. He reached over her head to grab an orange out of the basket on a higher shelf and slid a fingernail beneath the skin to start peeling. He made a small pile on a nearby counter with the rind and split the flesh in half. Char peeled one slice off and popped it into his mouth, chewing slowly to give her time to answer. When she didn't, he peeled off a second slice and held it out for her to take. She didn't hesitate, snatching it from his hand and stuffing it in her mouth as if afraid if she waited he would rescind the offer.

"How are you related to Karl?" Char repeated. He held out a third slice, which she grabbed and jammed into her already full mouth.

"M' sister," she mumbled, a line of juice running down her chin. She wiped the goop off with the back of her hand before holding it out to ask for another slice.

Char obliged, giving her two.

"Why are you here?" Char added.

She shrugged and swallowed. "Nowhere else to go."

So she had followed Karl here at some point, since he was probably her caretaker on the streets. Safer to be a hidden mouse here, than trying to survive so young without someone older to help. Char handed her the rest of the orange, reaching above her to a cloth-covered basket on the highest shelf where the leftover bread was stored. Some of it would be used to make egg toast for breakfast, some destined to become croutons, and Char was hoping to make a dressing with the remainder later in the week when he had plans to cook sliced turkey breast in gravy.

He pulled out a roll and went to the cold box where he found the open jar of apricot preserves. Char split the roll with a knife and slathered on the preserves. The orange was gone, and she was halfway through eating the apple, when Char handed her the sandwich.

"Right," Fen said. He dropped a gentle hand on her shoulder. "I think you, Karl, and I need to have a chat." He guided her in the direction of the doorway, but the heated look he shot over his shoulder at Char said he also wanted to have a chat about everything that had transpired before the girl's appearance.

Char quickly washed the knife and his teacup, shut off the lights, and followed them out of the dining hall. The hour was late, and he had to be awake again soon, and Char's heart was still thumping a touch too fast at the memory of kissing Fen.

Char needed to crawl into bed, shut his brain off, and think about everything that had happened over the last few days in the morning. Including that incredible, wonderful, mind-blowing kiss.

In the morning, Char thought sternly as he let himself into his room. That was soon enough to explore all the implications and to dream about where they might lead.

Chapter Fifteen

CHAR HEADED DOWN the hall toward his kitchen the next morning feeling somewhat refreshed. He had slept well, but the crazed, swirling thoughts had returned the second he opened his eyes. And he had definitely dreamed about that kiss.

He stomped firmly on that thought to prevent it from escalating before pushing open the doors. He walked into the kitchen and realized the lights were already on. He froze, looking around, one hand still holding open one of the doors in case he needed to make a run for it. Char noticed a man's silhouette out of the corner of his eye and a shot of adrenaline ran through him, but when he turned to look, Ralph's familiar face swam into view.

Char let out a heavy breath, his heart pounding in his chest. "What are you doing here?" he said, trying to sound nonchalant and not as if Ralph had just scared the crap out of him.

Ralph laughed. "I'm on guard shift in the mornings three days a week," he explained. "Means I have to get up early to beat you here, but I also get out of kitchen duty entirely so I really can't complain." He grinned. "And now I get to learn all about everything you complete before your helpers wander in."

Char laughed, the last of the tension draining out. "It's not much, really." He went to the ovens to get them lit so they could start to warm up. "I assume you didn't see anyone lurking in the dark when you got here this morning?" He pulled three extra-large stockpots down from the shelf and placed them on the stove before heading to the fridge to retrieve the milk. Yesterday afternoon, the dairy that supplied Char's kitchen had accidentally delivered double the milk of Char's usual order, and then when Char agreed to keep it rather than force them to lug it all the way back to the dairy where it would go bad before it could be sold, they had only charged him half price with no delivery fee. That meant he had more than enough milk to go a touch crazy with breakfast.

He filled all three pots two-thirds full with milk, added some salt, and left them there. It was far too early to start cooking, but that was one fewer step he now needed to complete.

"Not a soul," Ralph replied, shrugging. "They could have heard me coming and snuck out before I got the lights on though."

"Hmm," Char answered, mostly focused on measuring out oats to put in one of the pots. He was making oatmeal, creamed wheat, and break-fast grits to go with his cinnamon rolls. He would have Karl and one of his helpers set up a make-your-own bar with toppings and flavorings of all kinds to mix into the breakfast cereal. And, once he had a moment, he would also start making both fifteen minute hard boiled eggs and six-minute soft boiled as well.

Once the oats were measured, he set them aside. Char went over to the rack where the servants had placed all the raw bread to come to room temperature and pulled out the largest loaves first. The oven was hot enough, so those went in to start baking.

"Heard you caught a different sort of problem last night, though," Ralph continued.

Char snorted out a laugh, by now inured to the speed of the rumor mill around the compound. "Yeah, Karl's little sister paid us a visit. Caught her stealing an apple from the pantry."

While Ralph was busy chuckling, Char filled two medium stockpots about halfway with cold water and set them on the counter, then pulled out his eggs. He put fifty eggs in each pot, doused them liberally with salt, and put both pots on the stove with their burners on high to get the water boiling.

Next, he vanished into the pantry to pull out all the sides and set up an assembly line with the serving bowls for Karl and the rest of the early helpers to prepare. The morning bell went off, meaning they would arrive in the next fifteen to twenty minutes.

A check on the bread said it needed a few more minutes, so while he waited, Char got a massive chunk of butter out of the cold box and put it in a saucepot on the stove, heating on low to start melting. And then he paused, casting around, but there wasn't anything else to prep for breakfast.

He ought to start working on any prep for the next meal, then. Although lunch was going to be leftovers. Thinly sliced steak round—since that meat was a few days old and needed to be eaten—as well as the sliced chicken Char hadn't been able to use for the pot pie. If he had any leftover eggs after breakfast, he would also toss together some egg salad. The sand-wich bread was in the oven at the moment and throwing together a condi-ment of his spiced tomato sauce mixed with mayo would only take a few minutes. Yesterday's side salad and some sliced vegetables and he had a per-fect lunch. In the winter for a lunch like this, he would make a hearty soup too, but it was still far too warm for that.

Dinner was going to be hamburgers, so at some point this morning Char needed to make bun dough, but he didn't have enough time for that now.

Luckily Char's helpers started arriving before his indecision made him start working on something he didn't need to do right now. While they washed their hands and pulled on aprons, Char swapped the bread in the oven with the cinnamon rolls. The butter was melted, so he took it off the stove and set it aside to cool. He also turned the burners on for the milk, setting them on medium high. He poured the oats into one of the pots and found spoons to stir each.

"Hey, Char?" Karl asked, his tone tentative. Char turned to look at him and saw his sister was standing at his side. "Um, commander said she can stay if she contributes? Is there anything she can help with?"

She was still wearing the oversized white shirt as a dress, although the rope had been replaced with a proper leather belt. Both siblings looked so hopeful as they gazed at Char, and Char couldn't come up with any reason to say no.

"She can keep the milk from burning," Char said. "Karl, go get her a chair to stand on while I improvise an apron."

First, Char turned down the heat on the eggs, since they were just starting to boil, and glanced at the clock so he wouldn't overcook the soft-boiled ones. He then commandeered a drying cloth, poked holes in two of the corners, and used some twine to make a loop. The cloth hung awkwardly across her chest and stomach, but at least she would be protected from hot splashes.

"There's one spoon per pot," Char explained as Karl helped her climb onto the chair pressed up close to the stove. "Don't mix them up." He handed her the spoon for the oatmeal and she started stirring enthusiastically. Too enthusiastically, as some—thankfully still cool—milk immediately splashed. "Slowly! Slowly," Char admonished. "Use technique rather than speed. Scrape the spoon along the bottom of the pot to keep anything from sticking, and along the sides to keep anything from clumping. The milk is going to get hot, but when it starts to bubble and froth, call me over. You got it?"

She nodded, clutching the spoon in both hands as she stirred slowly and carefully. Char would keep an eye on her, but she seemed to get it. She put that spoon down on a spoon rest, picked up a different spoon and used it to stir the pot Char was going to use for the creamed wheat. He left her to it, beckoning Karl and Leslie over to his prep station. Char held out the mallet for Karl to take, then pointed at the waiting bag of walnuts.

"I need those crushed. Not powdered; small chunks, please. And if you hit too hard and break my counter, you'll be doing dishes the rest of your time here," Char added, only half joking.

Karl nodded, his eyes serious, and when he started banging at the nuts, he tapped slowly the first few times until he got the heft of the hammer. Char explained to Leslie what he wanted for the rest of the bowls before hurrying over to swap out the tray of cinnamon rolls.

By then, the six-minute eggs were done. Char hefted the pot over to the sink and put the full pot directly underneath the faucet to fill it to the brim with cold water. He waited until the pot overflowed, then dumped the water out—careful not to lose any of the eggs. He filled and dumped the pot a second time, before setting the now cooled pot down at the bottom of the sink and letting it fill a third time. He left it there and went to find a large serving bowl.

"Let them cool enough you don't burn yourself, and then get these plattered. They're soft-boiled, so if you break one we'll have a mess," Char explained to Marcus, who was standing nearby, waiting for instructions.

Marcus nodded and got to work, and Char went to make the icing for his buns. The first batch was going to be served plain, but the rest were getting a lovely coating of sweet goodness. Char combined the melted butter with powdered sugar, milk, and vanilla, stirring until he had a smooth, pourable mixture. That would go directly on the rolls when he pulled them out of the oven.

"Hey, Mister Char, sir?" Karl's sister called.

Char hurried over and saw the milk was boiling. "Good eye," he told her. Char measured the grits into one pot, the creamed wheat into another, and left her to stirring. The next round of cinnamon rolls was done. Char pulled them and slotted in the normal rolls Karl had made next. He iced the cinnamon rolls and then went to help set up the serving area.

Explaining how he wanted things arranged only took a few minutes, which was good because the hard-boiled eggs were done. He hauled the pot over to the sink, sticking it directly under the running faucet exactly as he had done for the soft-boiled eggs, only dumping it out when the water overflowed the edges. He filled and dumped the water three times before leaving the pot in the sink. Marcus was waiting again, so Char started explaining what he wanted done.

"These eggs are hard-boiled, so I need you to peel them," Char explained, picking up one of the warm eggs. Karl wandered over to watch too, apparently done helping Leslie. "You don't have to worry about a mess with these, but they're still very delicate, so I need you to be gentle." He demonstrated by tapping the egg against the side of the sink just hard enough to crack the shell. Using the outside edge of his thumb, careful not to scrape the white flesh with his nail, Char peeled the shell off. "See this membrane?" he explained, holding up a thin white film that had come up with the shell. "If it gets stuck to the egg the shell won't come off cleanly. See?" He demonstrated, gently peeling the membrane back with the edge of his thumb, revealing the unmarred egg underneath. "Any questions? Try not to rip out too much of the white flesh."

Marcus and Karl both nodded, reaching for their own eggs to give peeling a try. Char left his denuded egg in another serving bowl and left them to it, their delicate tapping of the cooked shells against the metal of the sink a pleasant accompaniment to the *blurp* and bubble of the breakfast cereals starting to come together just in time for the main doors to open for the first diners.

The rest of the morning passed in a blur of keeping the serving area full. The lull before the soldiers finishing morning drill was ending and Char was elbow deep in peeling even more hard-boiled eggs when Zain walked into the room. Her sheer presence drew the eye, even when she was simply walking to grab a plate, although she paused to take an appreciative sniff of the air. Heady with yeast and the sharp tang of cinnamon, Char sometimes thought the best thing about making cinnamon rolls was the way they perfumed the air, rather than how good they tasted. Zain apparently agreed, since she breathed heavily in and out a second time.

"Whoa," Karl's sister breathed out, awe suffusing her tone.

Zain looked up and caught sight of the girl still standing over a pot—a refill of oatmeal, since they were running low—spoon clutched in her hands.

"Girl, front and center," Zain snapped out, pointing at the ground in front of her.

Karl's sister gulped, and Karl sucked in a breath. It took her a second to set the spoon aside and climb down from the chair, but she went where directed.

"Name?" Zain asked.

"Em'ly," she replied. Her head was down and her shoulders rounded, and she was shaking like a chihuahua.

"Back straight! Look me in the eye when you're speaking to me, Emily," Zain snapped. Emily gasped but obeyed, standing straight and looking at Zain, her golden-colored eyes wide.

Zain nodded firmly. "You'll do. I'm Captain Patricia Zain. I'm in need of an aide. After I finish eating, report to me, and I'll put you to more appropriate work." She paused to wait for a response, but Emily only continued to stare. "You say, "Yes, Captain!""

"Yes, Cap Tin!"

Zain let out a snort and went to fill a plate, then headed off into the depths of the seats to sit with Captain Wong, who had come in about ten minutes earlier. Emily returned to the other side of the island and looked at Karl as if he had an answer to explain what just happened.

"I think she's only scary on the outside?" Karl asked more than said, turning to look at Char.

Char smiled. "Yes. She's a bit rough, but she'll treat Emily nicely. Just do what she says, and you'll be fine."

Emily took off her improvised apron and handed it to Char. She was still shaking and wide-eyed, but when Zain added her dishes to the collection bin and headed in the direction of the training courtyard outside, Emily trotted after her.

Karl returned the chair to the sitting area, Char took over oatmeal stirring duties, and the morning continued.

Chapter Sixteen

CHAR WAS FINISHING a brunoise dice on yellow onions when Fen walked into the kitchen. He hadn't been at breakfast or lunch, and there was still a good hour until dinner. He looked tired with pronounced circles under his eyes, but he smiled when he caught sight of Char.

"Hey, Char. Can I steal you away for ten minutes to talk?"

Fen looked serious, although he was still smiling, so Char knew he didn't want to have a conversation about that kiss. Or, at least, not only about that kiss. Something more was on his mind.

"Yes. Let me just…" he trailed off as he went to the oven and checked the buns. Luckily, they were done. Char pulled them out and set the tray on the cooling rack. Since he didn't know how long the meeting would take, Char didn't put the next tray in to start cooking. A glance around the kitchen showed everyone else was still occupied by their current tasks and wouldn't need anything from him for a while. Karl and Laura were by the sink, scrubbing potatoes. Mark was using the fry press to create fries from the cleaned potatoes. Char could cut the fries faster and better with a knife, but the press did an adequate job, so he focused his time on other tasks. Satisfied that he could leave for a while, Char left the onions on the cutting board, draped his apron over a clean bit of counter, and followed Fen out of the dining hall.

They went upstairs, an area Char didn't explore often. The hallway to the right of the landing had more doors for bedrooms, going all the way to the front of the building. To the left—the area above the dining hall and Char's kitchen—was another set of double doors, these propped open. Six desks filled the open area in the middle, all with what Char assumed were secretaries or aides working hard on the stacks of paperwork that appeared to be absolutely everywhere. The perimeter of the room had five closed doors, two each on the left and right, and one on the back wall. Fen led the way to the farthest door on the right. He held it open for Char and closed it after them before going to sit in the chair behind the desk dominating the center of the room. Char took one of the two chairs on the visitors' side and waited for Fen to explain.

"My mother sent Second Minister Protus," Fen blurted out in a sudden non-sequitur. "I wanted you to know that mystery has been solved—and dealt with," he added, a growl in his voice. "My mother sends her apologies for frightening you."

"Eh," Char mumbled unsure what he really wanted to ask first, or if he even had the right to ask. As usual, Fen understood him anyway.

Fen let out a long sigh. "I told my family I had feelings for you," he began, and Char's cheeks immediately flared with heat. Fen chuckled, but thankfully didn't comment. "My mother took it upon herself to test you and enlisted Protus. He's a career politician. However, despite how he comes across or what Karl might say, he's a good person. Karl might complain that he got six months for failing to pick Jensen's pocket, but in Protus's mind, six months is enough time for Karl to turn his life around. During that time, he'll be well-fed, housed, clothed, and taught a profession. Many of the street waifs sent to us join up when they've served their sentence and start a military career that keeps them off the streets permanently. Something I doubt Karl understands right now. Protus is also a good judge of character. He told Jensen he didn't notice any signs of subterfuge from you, nor the least bit of interest in his offer, which Protus then told my mother, who informed me she approved of you this morning when I met her for breakfast."

"Oh. Um, that's good?" Char got out, his cheeks flaming to the point they were probably measurable on the Scoville scale, his breath stuttering at the idea the queen knew all about him. Then, there was also the fact that Fen had told her about Char in the first place.

Fen's eyes crinkled at the corners, his smile growing. "So you don't need to worry about him any longer. We're still investigating the second person who threatened you, the one from early the next morning. I hope to have that one resolved soon as well.

"Now, about Emily Mitely. She doesn't have a legal guardian and her only family is Karl Mitely. If I send her back to the city, she'll go into a crown-funded orphanage. Technically that's better than being on the streets, but far too many of the orphans don't do well while there or after they age out. My mother's been fighting for improvements for the last decade, but it's a painfully slow battle that she hasn't won…yet. I figured Emily could stay here until we can find other arrangements, but I'm sorry I had to drop her in your lap."

Char shrugged, glad he had a different topic to focus on as that helped his face cool down. "A busy kitchen is no place for a child. Luckily, Zain took one look at her, and Emily is now with Zain for the afternoon. Not that I think a military training yard is an appropriate place either, but Zain was insistent."

Fen rubbed a hand over his eyes as he let out a sigh. "I see. Zain likes kids, particularly little girls. She has four boys; the fourth happened because she wanted to try one last time for a girl and failed. If Zain's taken charge of Emily, I won't worry about what to do about her any longer. Thanks for telling me." He paused to look at Char and all mirth vanished from his face. "What I'm about to tell you next doesn't leave this room, understand?" he asked.

Char nodded, gulping. "I understand."

Fen pinched the bridge of his nose with two fingers for a long moment before looking at Char again. Something sad lurked behind those usually vibrant hazel eyes, something that darkened them and made Char want to reach out to give Fen a hug or another form of comfort. Char could only listen and hope that even in silence he could convey his support.

"I don't know if you remember, but when Roe killed herself, she said, 'Randolph says hi.' Prince Randolph was my father's youngest sibling, born third in line for the throne. No one knows why or what might have instigated it, but Randolph was incredibly jealous and spiteful that he wasn't slated to be the next king. My father was crowned fifteen years ago. Five years later, Randolph staged a coup. His forces killed Aunt Stephanie and Ayer—um, Crown Prince Ayer—spent six months under a healer's care recovering from his injuries. The coup failed and Uncle Randolph fled.

Braxton and I spent the next few years stomping out small rebellions all over the country. That's how I became commander, actually, despite being the youngest of the captains at the time, by proving my abilities in all those skirmishes. About six years ago, Braxton's unit finally found where Uncle Randolph was hiding, and Braxton killed him in the resulting battle. We thought that ended it, but over the last year or so we started hearing whispers that while Randolph might be dead, his cause isn't. We believe Namin is behind it, since fomenting unrest in Toval would benefit them the most. We confirmed our suspicions when we captured Namin's Prince Clament directing the mercenary groups. I believe—and the rest of my family agrees—the dark stranger who threatened you is part of whatever is left of Randolph's coup." He paused as if to gauge Char's reaction, but Char was too stunned to respond.

He had been in school during the fighting, and Timmonsville considered itself neutral when it came to other countries' politics. At the time, Char was much more interested in learning how to fillet fish than about Toval's internal war, but he had heard there was some unrest. Plus, his cousin had gotten a job in Etoval around then, so some of the letters Char had received from his parents mentioned Terrance was safe in the palace kitchen, far away from any fighting. The majority of his family lived and worked in Toval, but in other cities and towns, so had stayed well away from the unrest. But that was all he really knew about any of it.

Now, he was apparently smack dab in the middle of the ongoing conflict.

"You shouldn't have any reason to worry any longer," Fen continued. He reached across the desk and took Char's hand, the warmth of his touch soothing. "You'll have a guard with you at all times during the day, and the soldiers on night duty have increased patrols around the barracks. As long as you let me or Jensen know any time you need to leave the military complex, no one can get to you here."

Char swallowed hard but nodded. "I really appreciate having someone guarding me, so thank you for that. I was planning to go to the market in Etoval next week to pick up some supplies for winter prep, but I can postpone that."

Fen grimaced before shaking his head. "No, hiding in fear won't help either. We need to present a strong front and show we're not going to cower behind our walls." He squeezed Char's hand. "We'll double your guard that day, and I'll put the city guards on notice. With a week to prepare, you should never be in danger."

Fen let out a slow, heavy breath, looking down at the surface of the desk. When he looked up again, his eyes were blazing, twin hazel-colored flames like caramel bubbling as the sugar melted. He stood and walked around the desk without letting go of Char's hand. He settled onto the corner next to Char and gripped Char's hand in both of his.

"I refuse to let anything happen to you. You understand?"

Char couldn't breathe, Fen's words and the heat in his eyes stealing away any coherent thoughts as Char stared, mouth gaping like a fish out of water. Fen's responding chuckle was deeper than normal, almost a growl from his chest. He bent forward and placed the barest peck on the corner of Char's mouth. He lifted one hand and gently closed Char's mouth and then bent close to press his lips square over Char's. This time when Fen pulled away, he trailed his fingertips across Char's cheek, and Char let out a mewling whimper.

Char surged forward, pressing his lips against Fen's in a third kiss, this one heavy with want and emotion blasting between them. When Fen's tongue brushed against Char's lip, Char opened, glad to give everything he had and take everything Fen offered in turn.

They were both panting for breath, lips swollen and wet, when they pulled apart.

"Dinner," Char explained, his voice breathy because he couldn't get enough oxygen to form more than the barest sounds.

Fen growled but nodded. "Tonight instead? When you're done for the night? My room is the door on the back wall of the outer office."

Char wanted to lean forward and get lost in another kiss, but he knew if he did, dinner would be comprised of a few dozen baked buns, raw dough, and diced yellow onion. His duty to put food on the table came first, just as Fen's duty as commander did as well. Char took in and let out two deep breaths, trying to calm his heartrate and libido. He dried his lips with the back of one hand and hoped his face didn't look too obvious as to what he and Fen had just been doing, before resolutely walking out the door and returning to the kitchen.

He scrubbed his hands at the sink, redonned his apron, and got back to work. The next round of buns went into the oven, the onions were chopped, the garlic cleaned, and Char knew he was damned lucky his magic was basically automatic at this point, because he would have burned the crap out of his hand or chopped off a finger in his distraction without that protection. For the first time in Char's memory, he couldn't properly focus on cooking while in the kitchen in the midst of meal prep.

Every inch of him yearned to return upstairs and to see where those three brief kisses might lead if given plenty of time to explore those possibilities. Pulling pounds upon pounds of ground beef out of the cold box was a poor distraction, but that was all Char had.

He forced himself to refocus as he split the beef in half. For the first half, he pulled individual portions off the lump of meat and rolled each first into a loose ball and then flattened it into a disk, careful not to press too hard and turn the disk into a puck that wouldn't cook properly. Each patty then got a light dusting of garlic and onion powder on both sides. A glance at the clock said Char was running late, so the patties went directly onto the grill. Once the grill was full, Char continued making and dusting patties, placing them onto a plate instead, until that half of the beef was gone. Then he moved onto the other half, which he dumped into a large bowl.

"Anything I can help with?" Karl asked as he wandered over.

"Mushrooms done?" Char asked, glancing over at the sink where a bowl of cleaned white button mushrooms was waiting for him to find five minutes to slice.

"All cleaned."

Karl grinned at Char, but his smile turned into a quizzical look a moment later when Char dumped the onions into the bowl of meat. Char used a garlic press to mince the garlic cloves, added chopped basil and parsley and some salt, and then started cracking eggs into the bowl. Once he had enough eggs, Char added his lightly spiced tomato dipping sauce and topped it off with cracker meal—a substance made from finely ground crackers that served as a binder.

"Let me see your hands," Char asked Karl as he measured the last of the cracker meal into the bowl.

Karl held his hands up for Char to see, a quizzical look on his face. His fingers were slightly damp, but clean after spending so much time at the sink. There was no need to make him wash them again.

"Can you mix this for me?" Char asked as he headed back to the grill to flip patties.

"Sure. Do you have a spoon?" Karl asked, glancing around to see if Char had left one nearby.

Char laughed. "No spoon for this recipe. Dig in with your hands so you can get everything properly incorporated."

"Nice!" Karl exclaimed, immediately digging into the bowl with both hands, meat and liquids squelching between his fingers.

Char left him to it, moving on to the mushrooms. He diced the white buttons, pausing halfway through to remove the medium-rare patties from the grill, load up another round, and start oil heating for the potato fries. The mushrooms went into a pan with oil to start reducing. Once they had lost most of their water and were starting to darken, Char added red wine, Worcestershire sauce, onion, garlic, and a dash of red pepper powder, then covered the pan to let them simmer on low heat until Char was ready to serve. He exchanged cooked buns for raw in the oven and then pulled out a large bag full of gigantic portabella mushrooms marinating in oil, white wine vinegar, and spices. He filled the grill with those next, the trimmed stem side up to form a bowl for the marinade to pool as they cooked. While Char didn't have any vegetarians to feed, some people liked the taste of a portabella either in addition to or instead of a beef burger.

Finally, Char was able to return to Karl, looking over Karl's shoulder at the mixture in the bowl, which was slightly too wet. Char added more cracker meal for Karl to mix in. If it had been too dry, he would have added more tomato sauce. By the time the portabellas were flipped and fully cooked, Karl had finished mixing and Char was able to start forming patties. They went right on the flat iron—the consistency was too soft for the grill, since the meat would break apart and fall through the bars—where they would cook until well-done to ensure there was no chance of anyone eating raw eggs. These patties were meant to be eaten without a bun by using a fork to dip portions into tomato sauce.

And still, despite all the distractions, Char's lips were tingling in memory, and his mind was upstairs. Dinner service couldn't end soon enough.

Somehow, he did make it through. As the first rush of diners arrived and the scramble to keep the serving area full commenced, Char finally dragged his brain to focus on work. However, it only lasted until the final lull, when the compound began to quiet as people headed to their evening pursuits or to bed. Char started on his bread dough for the morning, his hands and wrists automatically going through the motions of mixing and kneading, the word "bed" echoing through his thoughts.

"Can I try?" Karl suddenly asked, breaking into Char's thoughts. He looked earnest and hopeful, so Char smiled as he stepped to the side.

"We're developing the glutens when we're kneading," Char explained. "Adding elasticity to our dough so it will rise better. Too little kneading and it won't develop. Too much and the bread turns into a rock." Char demonstrated the push, turn, push he used for this particular dough and then waved for Karl to try. "Not too hard; we don't want to break the dough when we're kneading either."

Karl nodded, concentrating hard on pushing the dough far enough to stretch it without breaking. His hands were smaller and he didn't have muscles built up in his forearms or wrists, so he was slower than Char, but he was working hard. Char left him to it, starting to mix together another dough. With Karl's help, the last of the evening chores were done early. Char sent his helpers off to bed, thanked his nighttime guard, and went to grab a shower.

Clean and dressed in a fresh set of clothes, Char swallowed hard and started climbing the staircase up to an evening he hoped would be as good as those kisses portended.

Chapter Seventeen

CHAR STRETCHED SLOWLY, full body from toes to head, pressing his fingertips against the headboard so his shoulders cracked. His body was sore but languid. Sated and comfortable with only the occasional twinge to remind him how long it had been since he last had a partner in bed. And yet, this time was different. All the previous partners had left a hollow feeling inside, an emptiness that only served to encourage Char to go find his own bed once the fun was over. This time he was laying in the same bed hours later, Fen's muscular arm thrown across his chest, still warm and tingly. And he was feeling happy too—bubbly, as if the first fizz of a bottle of soda water was erupting inside.

Unfortunately, Char's inner clock moved forward no matter how much he wanted to luxuriate in all those emotions. He had bread to get in the oven and breakfast to prepare, and his body had punted him awake at the normal hour regardless of his overnight exertions. Char stifled a groan and crawled out of bed quietly so he didn't wake Fen, who was breathing deeply despite being face down in his pillow.

Fen had a private bathroom in a small room off his bedroom. A perk of being commander, Char assumed, and it also explained why, after that first day, Char had managed to avoid running into a naked Fen showering again. Char quickly rinsed his body and shamelessly stole one of Fen's towels to dry off. After getting dressed—which took a while since his socks had somehow ended up on both sides of the bed—Char left the bedroom, walked through Fen's private sitting room, and out into the space with the desks for secretaries and aides. The room was dark and empty, echoing cavernously as Char crept through as if making a walk of shame. But he wasn't the least bit ashamed of last night, nor did he particularly care whether the entire army knew. All he cared about was getting to work on time, yet the predawn silence invoked such ridiculous thoughts. The birds weren't even chirping yet, since the sun was rising later and later every morning as autumn started to really hint at the coming winter.

Char made it downstairs and into his brightly lit kitchen without incident. Ralph's smirk was knowing as he waved hello from where he was sitting at one of the tables.

"The night guards apparently had a moment of panic when they realized you weren't in your room last night," Ralph called as Char lit the ovens. "Luckily, Emmerson saw you heading upstairs before someone decided to sound an alarm and accidentally interrupt the commander's evening." He waggled his eyebrows meaningfully, still grinning a touch too widely.

Char gave him a look over the counter. "Do you want breakfast today or not?" he asked, his tone somewhere between stern and joking, since he wasn't sure whether he wanted to scowl or laugh at Ralph's commentary.

Ralph snickered, holding up his hands defensively. "Please don't burn the bread because of me."

Char sniffed, putting his nose in the air and definitely joking now. "My bread is always perfect, thank you very much."

This was the slow morning of the week when the majority of the royal guard were at morning drill. Char was going to offer make-your-own egg sandwiches, this time with freshly poached eggs on Timmons muffins, a flat, airy muffin perfect for making sandwiches. Most would have runny yolks; however, he would make some with solid yolks for diners who preferred not to have the mess of yolk running everywhere. A delicious mess, for certain, but not conducive to carrying or eating neatly. A couple of cheese options and other things to add into the sandwich, and the main component of breakfast would be done. And then he would make muffins to tide over everyone finishing morning drill until the massive lunch rush.

Char slotted the first trays of bread into the oven and vanished into the pantry to collect his ingredients for muffins. When he emerged, the first of his helpers was walking into the kitchen. The rest followed soon after. And then Karl arrived. Char expected Emily would be with him, but not the second boy also sheepishly standing behind Karl, as if Karl's body could shield him somehow. He was wearing the usual uniform of white shirt and brown pants. He had light brown hair and eyes, a smattering of freckles across his nose, and appeared to be a year or two younger than Karl.

"Who's this?" Char asked.

At the same time, Ralph groaned out, "They're multiplying!"

"This is Shan," Karl explained. "He can contribute too!"

Char snapped his mouth shut, but before he could come up with something to say, Zain blew into the room, her footsteps slapping with command against the tiled floor. She was wearing her leather practice armor and cut an authoritative figure that had all three kids staring at her.

"I arranged school for you two." She paused as she caught sight of Shan, then amended her statement. "For you three. You'll be attending with my youngest son. Be ready to leave at eight. Emily, with me." She headed off, taking her aura of authority with her, going outside where she could terrorize the troops through morning drill, Emily trotting in her wake.

Since the decision on whether Shan was staying had just been neatly taken out of Char's hands, he shrugged and let it go.

"How can you contribute, Shan? Do you know anything about cooking?"

Shan first shook his head, then nodded. "Not food, but I'm real good with knives. I think I'd like sticking a knife in a potato more than in a guy's belly though."

Char very much did not want to know, so he didn't ask. Ralph opened his mouth, then closed it while shaking his head, so apparently he didn't want to know either.

"Potatoes it is," Char finally said, since home fries would be a good accompaniment to the egg sandwiches. "Karl, I need thirty-five potatoes and ten onions cleaned. Shan, I'll show you how to cut the potatoes as soon as they're ready, so why don't you help Karl clean them for a bit?"

Char got everyone else situated at their tasks and returned to making muffins and cooking the bread. About twenty minutes passed before Shan walked over.

"Um, Mr. Char, sir?"

"Call him Chef!" Karl yelled over the sound of splashing water at the sink, where he was scrubbing potatoes.

"Um, Chef, we have lots of potatoes ready," Shan continued.

Char dusted the flour off his hands and went to retrieve two knives—one from his personal set, and the second for Shan to use from the kitchen set.

"Curl your fingers into a cat's paw," Char explained, demonstrating with the hand holding one of the damp potatoes in place on a cutting board. "That way you don't cut yourself."

"Oh, I don't have to worry about that!" Shan exclaimed. He grabbed the other knife and sliced it across his palm before Char could do more than let out a yelp. His palm flared with magic, a blue-green mix that said Shan hadn't settled on whether he wanted to go the route of the household—blue—or of the body—green. When he pulled the knife away, he was uninjured.

"I see," Char said, trying to channel what he remembered of the magic tutor his parents had hired when Char was about Shan's age. "Magic is very useful and the fact that you know how to use it to protect yourself is impressive, but magic has limitations. It is not an endless well of power inside you, and it will run out. If you do not learn how to use a knife correctly, what will you do when your magic reserves are empty, and you're asked to slice potatoes again?"

Shan was definitely a street kid, probably in the same gang or group as Karl. What had Char confused, though, was that he didn't have to be. Children with magic were sent to special schools to train them at the expense of the crown, particularly the children from poorer families that couldn't afford the private tutors Char's family had provided him. All schools in Toval were crown-funded, but the magic ones specialized not only in teaching children to use their magic, but also in helping them find employment after graduation. Shan should have jumped at the chance to attend, yet here he was instead. Shan's background was definitely mysterious, but it wasn't Char's mystery to solve. If Shan was going to be Char's responsibility in the kitchen—when he wasn't in school per Zain's orders—then at the very least Char was going to ensure Shan knew what he was doing.

Shan pursed his lips as he thought, and then he let out a little sigh. "I'd probably cut myself and bleed lots. So, a cat's paw?" He placed his hand on a second potato, his fingers curled.

Char showed him how to do a medium dice. "Slowly. Speed is not the goal. You want the pieces to all be the same shape to ensure they cook evenly, which is much more important than cutting quickly."

Char watched Shan slice at the potato. He was slower than Char but fairly precise. Speed would come with practice, and Char was impressed by how evenly shaped Shan's dice was. The only problem was every time Shan sank the knife into a cut, his magic flared in a bright blast, strobing in the room.

"You need to be slow with your magic too," Char said, his voice going deeper as he reached for the meditative chant that was almost second nature at this point. "Breathe in...and out...and in...and out..." Char continued, saying the words at a smooth beat, gratified when Shan followed the instructions perfectly. The pace of his cutting moderated to match his breathing. "Pull the magic evenly in a constant flow," Char said, still at the same cadence. "Let it coat your hand in a thin glove." The flaring slowed and then dimmed until Shan's hand glowed with a constant light. The power was more like a gauntlet than a glove, too thick and uneven, but Shan had the idea of it now. Like his cutting, he would improve with practice.

Char returned to his bread and muffins. When he paused to get a large pot of salted water and vinegar boiling for the eggs and to fill a deep-sided skillet with oil for the fries, a quick check on Shan showed he was still doing well.

The morning passed quickly, and it wasn't too long before the first diners began trickling in. Char was distracted with poaching eggs, but he still looked up almost instinctively when Fen walked in.

Fen immediately looked over at Char. His lips lifted just the slightest at the corners, and his eyes twinkled. Char's cheeks heated, and he ducked his head, looking down at the raw egg he had just cracked into the custard cup in his hand. He gave the simmering water in the pot on the stove between them a spin with a spoon to renew the swirling vortex before gently lowering the custard cup and pouring the egg into the water to begin cooking. In the half second that took, Char's cheeks cooled enough he felt safe looking up again.

Fen was closer, heading toward the end of the serving area to retrieve a plate. Still smiling at Char, his eyes crinkled at the corners, and the heat in Char's cheeks flared back up. Fen reached out to grab a plate but paused with his hand in midair to glance over his shoulder. Char noted the silence and followed his gaze, blinking as nearly every single person sitting at the dining tables abruptly looked away or averted their eyes. The general din of conversation picked back up, and Char's cheeks hit the Scoville scale again as he realized everyone had been watching them interact. When Fen looked back at Char, he winked and finally picked up a plate. Except, when he turned to look at the food on offer, he slowly put the plate back down. Char had sent Karl and Shan to eat a minute ago so they would be ready to leave for school on time, and the two of them were busy filling their plates exactly where Fen could see them.

"You two, with me!" Fen barked out, pointing first at Karl and Shan and then at the ground directly in front of him. The boys obeyed, leaving their plates in the serving area as they shuffled over to Fen.

"Who are you and how did you get here?" Fen asked, his voice only marginally quieter and still as stern and unyielding.

"Um, sir, this is Shan," Karl explained, gulping, both boys shivering under Fen's glare. "Err, Shannen Mitely. It was just us. Him, me, and Emily. And then I ended up here, and Shan helped get Emily safe, so I hoped I could help Shan too? He snuck in when the guard at the gate took his nighttime pee break, same as Emily."

Fen let out a very slow, very heavy breath and pinched the bridge of his nose for a long moment. He looked at Char. "Who approved him staying here?"

"Captain Zain, when she saw him this morning," Char replied immediately.

"Right. Of course. Thanks," Fen replied, letting out another heavy breath.

As if summoned, Zain blew into the room. Emily bobbed along in her wake like a duckling chasing after its mother. Zain caught sight of Fen interrogating Karl and Shan and arrowed in their direction.

"You approved another child?" Fen snapped.

Zain let out a snort. "I need my soldiers at drill where they belong," she snapped back, pointing at the woman from her unit who was currently elbow deep in soapsuds at the dishwashing station. "Your pretty chef needs extra pairs of hands. Giving him this kid solves both our problems. What's the big deal?"

This time Fen's heavy breath was a sharp inhale. "My office, 1400," he told her, his voice tight with suppressed fury. He turned to look at Karl and Shan. "Are any more of your friends going to appear here?"

"No, sir!" Karl replied.

"Fine. Go eat. You're dismissed," he added sharply to Zain. Karl and Shan returned to their plates. Zain picked up two empty ones and went down the line filling them. She plonked Emily down at the same table as her brother and went to sit with the officers. And Fen stood in the same place, purposefully taking even breaths as he fought to get his seething temper under control.

When Zain was seated, Jenson came over. "I'll get in touch with logistics, see about getting the kid properly authorized to be here." He paused, frowning. "Did Karl say the gate guard takes a regular nighttime pee break?"

"Yes. Yes, he did," Fen replied through gritted teeth, his voice softer now that he wasn't trying to make a point.

"They, um, don't get breaks. Right?"

"They remain at their post until their replacement arrives, or they follow the strictly outlined protocol if they need to step away. I'm going to eat something, and then I'm going to go have a very illuminating chat with the commander of the guard squad. I appreciate your taking the lead on coordinating with logistics. Take Emmerson with you. He's the secretary that straightened out the paperwork allowing Emily to stay here yesterday, so he already knows how to browbeat the penny-pinchers over there into submission."

"Will do." Jensen saluted and trotted off.

Fen sent Char a tight smile that said he would catch up with Char later and finally went to fill his plate. Char left to rescue his overboiled eggs, and the day continued from there.

Chapter Eighteen

A WEEK AND a half slid past far too quickly, and Char had practically moved into Fen's set of rooms. He hadn't meant to, but as every evening rolled around and Char finished closing up the kitchen for the night, he gravitated up the stairs and into Fen's space. And it was good. Very, very good in every salacious euphemism Char's brain could come up with. Even the nights Fen didn't make it to bed—too busy with work or because he was over at the palace until late and slept there—it was still good. Being surrounded by Fen, his musky scent from the soap in his shower and the earthy tang beneath enveloping Char, even when Fen's arms weren't there to hold Char close, gave a real sense of comfort and security.

Of course, the entire base knew. By the second day, Char found his clothes hanging in the closet—distinguishable from Fen's because they were two sizes smaller—and extra towels in the bathroom. Char wouldn't be surprised if the rest of his things and even some of his furniture began magically gravitating into Fen's rooms—the servants were scarily efficient—until Fen's rooms became *their* rooms. Perhaps that idea was the best part of all; the feeling of combining their lives together so viscerally and with the tacit support of everyone around them.

Unfortunately, this morning those good feelings were tenuous at best and fleeing quickly. For the first time since Char had been threatened by that dark stranger in his kitchen, he was leaving the security of the base to go to the market in the capital city. Char sat on the edge of the bed to pull his socks on and then paused, biting his lip as worries swirled through his mind.

Fen's gentle breathing behind Char slowed, and then Fen rolled over and wrapped his arms around Char's waist.

"You'll have two royal guards with you, and two more guards maintaining a perimeter," Fen explained, his lips moving against the back of Char's neck, feathering like butterfly wings. He pressed a kiss there before drawing back and shifting so he was sitting next to Char on the edge of the bed. "The city guards have been put on alert and have promised to increase patrols. Anyone who even thinks about targeting you will see all your protection and immediately cancel their nefarious plans. You'll be fine."

"I hope so." Char let out a sigh, wishing the churning feeling in his gut would be reassured by Fen's confidence.

"Oh! Before I forget. The quartermaster asked you to stop by if you have time today once you're back. He wants to measure you for winter gear."

"I won't need heavy clothes with the ovens blasting in the kitchen," Char said, wondering why a chef would need something like that.

Fen laughed. "This is the royal guard. At some point you're going to be deployed with us in the field again, and if it happens in winter the quartermaster wants to be prepared. Besides, you'll still be going to market in the winter, and there's the winter festivals and such. You'll need heavier gear for that too."

"I guess I will," Char replied. As usual, he hadn't thought much past the needs of his kitchen, but Fen had yet again easily compensated for him.

Fen leaned close, Char tilted his head, and their lips brushed briefly, a quick zing like the moment sweetness overtook the sour in that first gulp of lemonade. Fen drew away, leaving Char blinking in surprise and wanting more.

"You have bread to bake," Fen explained. "I'm going to the palace today, so I'll see you in the courtyard later."

The call of bread was stronger than the pull of Fen's smile, but only because Fen went into the bathroom and vanished from view. Char hurried downstairs and into the kitchen, waved to Ralph, and went to get the ovens lit. His helpers trickled in, but this time Char left them to their own thing, concentrating on the bread and only the bread. The cold and ice boxes were full of carefully labeled leftovers, each with detailed reheating instructions, and Char had trained enough people on the basic use of the kitchen, so he wasn't too concerned about returning to a disaster. Char had also heard the day's helpers were specifically chosen because they were competent in the kitchen since Char wasn't going to be around again until after the dinner rush to supervise.

Karl, Shan, and Emily wandered in, and Karl immediately went over to Char while the other two held back, looking anxious.

"Today is an off day from school," Karl began, standing back as Char pulled cooked bread from the oven and slotted in his last trays of raw. "And we made sure to finish our homework last night. Can we come with you to the city?"

"I can carry lots of stuffs for you!" Emily chimed in eagerly.

"Um," Char said, unwilling to commit to anything when it came to the three kids, particularly since Karl was technically here as punishment and might not be allowed to leave to go to the city. Ralph shrugged when Char glanced at him for help. "Tell you what," Char said, coming to a decision. "You can come out to the courtyard with me where Commander Fen will be waiting. If the commander says you can go, I'll allow it, but if he says no, you'll have to see if one of the captains could use you for the day instead."

Karl grinned. "Thanks, Chef!"

"Thanks!" the other two added.

Char sighed but let it go. He put together five plates from the leftovers the helpers were preparing, and he and the kids joined Ralph at a table to eat. By the time they were done, the last of the bread was also ready. Char left it to cool, wished the kitchen helpers luck, and led the way out of the kitchen, through the barracks, and out the front door. The walk to the courtyard didn't take too long, even when compensating for Emily's shorter stride, so soon enough they joined the small throng of people and horses.

Fen was waiting by Char's donkey—the same donkey from their trip over the mountains, who appeared to be happy to only be working during Char's market runs—so Char headed over there.

"Here ye are," a hostler said when Char reached Fen's side. "Yer donkey and the empty saddle bags. I know he's technically your beast, but we've taken to calling him Wise—" He cut off at the sight of the three kids behind Char and amended the second half of the name with barely a hiccup."—One. Hope you don't mind."

"Wise *One* is a great name for a donkey," Char replied, taking the reins from the hostler with a smile. "Thank you for getting him ready."

"Of course. Chef. Commander." He saluted them both before trotting off.

Bemused at being saluted, it took Char a moment to realize Fen was frowning at Karl, Shan, and Emily rather than after the hostler.

"If you go with Char, you're going to be part of his security detail. You understand?" Fen asked them, his voice stern and unyielding. "You will coordinate your actions with Sergeant Ralph and behave yourselves. You're representing the royal guard, and I expect you to act accordingly."

All three kids nodded solemnly, Emily's eyes as wide as saucers.

"Right. Let's mount up and get going." Fen shared a brief, private smile with Char before heading in the direction of the waiting horses. Char was going on foot, since even the donkey was technically too much to take into the busy market, but Fen kept the horses to a walk so they stayed together as they left the compound. Only when they reached the fork in the road where Fen went toward the palace did they separate. Char waved but continued onward in the direction of the main city gates.

Emily rode on the donkey, Karl and Shan walking on either side. Ralph was in front and Sherri in back. They maintained that formation even as they entered the line of people waiting to be admitted at the gates. Luckily, Ralph showed something to one of the guards so they bypassed the line, going into the city much faster than Char was used to when he went by himself.

The main city market was only about ten blocks into the city, close to the gate for merchants and farmers to come and go with ease and along the wide thoroughfare that cut through the center of the city. The morning was still young enough the crowds hadn't yet emerged, the current smattering of people nothing in comparison to what the crush would be when they left in a few hours.

Char ran through his mental list of what he wanted to buy. A couple hundred canning jars would be his main purchase—which he would have delivered since Wise One wouldn't be able to carry those in his saddle bags—but Char also wanted to start stocking up on high quality dried ingredients. Merchants would offer their wares and their business cards at the market, and Char would buy enough to experiment with the options before contracting for a regular delivery with the merchant directly. He also wanted to find some quality extra-large soup pots to supplement what the kitchen already had on hand since he hoped to serve soups and stews all winter at both lunch and dinner.

They traveled for about three blocks before Ralph swore quietly and stopped, his hand resting on the hilt of his sword. Char glanced around, gulping. At first glance, the twenty or so people surrounding them looked like other shoppers heading to the market. Yet, something about the way they stood read like a formation—too organized to be a coincidence. Plus, they stopped when Ralph stopped, and then suddenly drew their weapons and charged, not waiting for Ralph to finish drawing his sword.

After that day in the tent, all those weeks ago, when Char had learned he could use his magic to stop bladed weapons, he had practiced. Mostly by himself in the late evenings and never against an actual opponent, he was good at calling the magic to his arms or chest where he could more effectively shield himself. He coated himself now, glowing blue just in time, as a long knife was thrust in his direction.

Char blocked with his forearm, sending the knife wide to his left, and then shoved the attacker, who went sprawling and knocking over a couple more attackers as he fell. That wasn't nearly enough to help stem the quantity of people. Sherri was fighting at least five on her own, but they were effectively drawing her farther away from the group as they circled her. Char blocked and shoved a second time, but this time the attacker only fell back a single step before charging again. Emily rolled off Wise One with a shout and suddenly Shan was there, a knife in each hand, jabbing and slashing at the attackers like he knew what he was doing. Emily resurfaced from the scrum holding a knife, which she promptly sank into the nearest calf, thrusting with her whole body behind the move in a trained motion that Zain must have taught her.

Ralph had taken on nearly ten attackers, trying to draw the main group to him and away from Char. He was holding his own even against those odds, although Karl popped in and out of view, a pair of knives in his hands, helping to even the playing field.

Then, in the next moment, a flash of red magic erupted next to Ralph, who let out a pained shriek and went down.

"Ralp—" Char tried to yell, but then dark fabric dropped over his head. A *pop* sounded, blasting what felt like a sickly sweet-smelling powder all over his face, and then…nothing.

Interlude

THE BREAKFAST ROOM was as full as usual when Fen walked inside, except for Braxton's seat, which was empty. Mother looked up and smiled when she caught sight of Fen and waved one hand toward Fen's usual spot.

"I wasn't certain you were stopping by this morning," she said. "Weren't you taking a contingent of your newer recruits into the woods for wilderness training?"

Fen shrugged. "Captain Wong volunteered since most of the new recruits are in his unit."

"You usually join them anyway as a show of solidarity. The commander leads from the front," Ayer began, but then he paused and shared a smirk with Shairon. "Ah, your chef is in the city today. I forgot."

Shairon nodded, still smirking jovially. "It's market day. Our dear brother wouldn't dare be miles away, lost in a forest, when his pretty chef might be in peril."

"I assume you took precautions?" Mother asked. "And sit, down, dear. You're not addressing the military council."

Fen sat and then waited while servants placed a plate in front of him—scrambled eggs, toast, cut fruit, and an assortment of jams—and poured him some tea. He took a bite and stifled a sigh, wondering if he could have Char stop by the kitchens on the mornings Fen was going to eat breakfast at the palace. Fen had no idea what was missing from the eggs, but they definitely didn't taste as good as when Char served them.

"I took plenty of precautions," Fen began after he swallowed his first bite. "The city guard knows this is an opportunity to catch any Namin spies trailing after Char, so they're on high alert. Plus, I sent Sergeant Ralph with Char."

"Isn't Sergeant Ralph the one who beat Braxton at that tournament last year? He's incredibly skilled," Ayer asked.

Fen nodded. "He's the best of my elite royal guards. When Captain Plairis retires within the next few years and his second takes the captain role, I'm going to recommend Ralph to fill her spot. Although, speaking of Braxton, where did that brat run off to? I wanted to ask him about the man he sent to that border town where we thought Namin forces might be holing up."

Ayer shrugged, but Father was the one who answered. "Something came up with the Namin prince you have stashed in my dungeons. Braxton wasn't clear. Hopefully this means the boy is ready to talk, but he's held out this long, so I doubt it. I'll have Braxton report to you at the military compound if he's found anything about that village."

"I appreciate it," Fen replied. He tucked into the rest of his breakfast and let the inane chatter of his family distract him. Fen wanted to be in the city, exploring the market at Char's side, but he didn't dare. Everyone in the military complex might know he and Char were in a relationship—which meant everyone in the country would shortly know too, since soldiers and gossip went hand in hand—but making it overt by appearing in public with Char would cement those rumors into fact. At a time when Namin was attempting to ferment unrest using Uncle Randolph's name, physically seeing Fen with Char would make Char far too tempting a target. With gritted teeth, he sat and listened to stories from Sammie—Ayer's oldest—about her tutors and learning magic and such. The words washed over him, and Fen sat back in his chair to finish his tea. Once breakfast was over, the kids would be sent away with their nurses and tutors so the adults could take care of real business, so Fen just had to be patient for a little longer.

The door slammed open, making Fen jump and spin around, already halfway out of his chair with a hand on his sword hilt. The two palace guardsmen stationed outside the door stumbled inside, followed by two men wearing the city guard uniform. Between them, they held up a battered woman, the left side of her face so swollen and purple it took Fen a second to recognize Sherri.

"Ambush, Commander," she forced out, each word accompanied by a hiss of pain. "Kidnapped Chef and Sergeant."

Fen was on his feet, his mind buzzing and his hands shaking. His mouth moved, but no words came out.

"How?" Ayer asked, suddenly appearing at Fen's side.

"It was fast," one of the city guards explained. Shairon brought over a chair and they gently sat Sherri down, and she hissed in a way that said she had some broken ribs. "In and out in less than three minutes. They attacked, a group separated your soldier here from the rest," he said with a wave at Sherri. "Don't know how they got the other one, but he fought like a demon and then suddenly went down. The group bundled up your chef and soldier and vanished down an alley as we were running to provide support. We pursued, but they were gone. They left behind their wounded and dead, though, so we'll know more as soon as we finish searching the bodies and conducting interrogations."

"And the kids?" Fen heard his voice ask as if from a great distance.

"Got away," Sherri hissed out.

"Damned good fighters, those kids," the city guard added. "But the second they saw the chef was taken, they ran off too."

At least threatening to harm the kids couldn't be used to force Char into compliance, a dry, clinical, and calculating part of Fen's brain supplied. Of course, that could explain why they took Ralph too, rather than leaving him like they had their own wounded—because Ralph would have to be wounded, but not dead, to explain how they were able to take him and why they would bother.

"Two of our citizens were kidnapped in the middle of our city?" Father asked, standing. All four soldiers immediately bowed, and Sherri swayed forward in her chair before Mother gently pressed her back. "Organize a door-to-door search. I want the culprits found and our citizens rescued. Fen, take charge. Someone get this soldier to a healer."

People went running. Fen shook his head, trying to make the buzzing stop, then nodded to his father.

"I'll be in the city. Let me know if you hear anything," he said. He didn't wait for a response before hurrying out the door. He would find Char. He had to. And, hopefully, before it was too late.

Chapter Nineteen

CHAR DRIFTED BACK to consciousness slowly, feeling like his brain was swimming through syrup. He quickly realized he was sitting on a hard chair, but it took him a while for his brain to engage enough to understand the reason he was upright was because of ropes tied around his chest, holding him to the chairback. His arms were tied at the wrists behind the chair, and his ankles were tied to the chair legs.

Whatever was draped over his head vanished with a yank, and Char squinted in the sudden brightness of the overhead mage lights. Char blinked to clear his vision as someone stepped into view. The familiar dark-shrouded person from his kitchen all those mornings ago stood in front of Char, arms crossed over their chest.

"I warned you I would be back to hear your answer," they said, voice harsh and cold. "This is a mere example of the strength we can bring to bear. Agree to our terms, and you can walk out of here right now, unharmed. Choose to be difficult, and you won't like what might happen to you. Something similar to what we're doing to your friend."

They glanced up, over Char's head, and a second later a scream echoed through the room, followed by whoever it was gasping for breath.

"Who—?" Char cut himself off because that had to be Ralph. The scream was low and masculine, definitely adult.

"Your poor guard thought he could protect you. Instead, we'll be happy to use his pain to ensure your compliance." They paused, looking at something else behind Char, and shrugged. "You're in luck," they finally said. "I've been called away. I will give you a few minutes to think it over. I will return very soon, so don't fret for long."

They walked around Char, and a moment later, hinges squeaked as a door whooshed open. It clicked closed and a *thunk* indicated a bar was dropped to lock the door again.

Char waited, craning his neck around to try to see if the dark person was just trying to trick him. He didn't see or hear anyone though.

"Ralph, are you okay?" Char called, unsure how loud he dared raise his voice.

"I've been better," Ralph replied, his voice tight. "Can you loosen your ropes at all?"

Char wiggled his arms, trying to loosen the ropes around his wrists. All he got was rope burn for his efforts. He opened his mouth to tell Ralph, and then snapped it shut again when the clunk of the bar being removed from the door sounded. Barely two minutes had passed since the dark person had left! Couldn't they give Char a few more minutes to wallow and panic?

Yet the voices Char heard next definitely did not belong to the stranger.

"Is it clear?" Shan hissed.

"I don't see anyone," Karl whispered back.

The scuttle of small feet sounded next, and then Karl's grinning face appeared in front of Char.

"We've got you, Chef. Quick," he added to Shan behind Char. The cold press of a knife slid against Char's wrist, and then the ropes dropped free. Karl bent to free Char's ankles, while Shan cut the ropes holding Char's chest, and Char stood. He rubbed at his wrists as he hurried over to where Ralph was lying against the wall, a few feet from the door. Emily had cut his ropes and was yanking on his hands to help him sit up.

"Can you stand?" Karl asked Ralph.

Ralph shook his head. "I just need a few minutes. You four go ahead, and I'll catch up."

The lie didn't land on any of them, Karl crossing his arms and Shan frowning even more than Char.

"You can lean on me," Char said, reaching out to help Ralph to his feet, and then he caught sight of Ralph's leg. His pants had been sliced open and what was left of the cloth hung in shreds, leaving the injury open to the air. White and yellow pus oozed out of the cut on his thigh, the skin around it streaked purple and red, pulsing and swollen.

"I can fix that!" Emily chirped. Her hands suddenly glowed green, and Char stifled a gasp. She had magic too? And healing magic, which definitely ensured she would be well taken care of both in school and in employment afterward. What the heck was she doing on the streets with Shan? The swelling on Ralph's leg shrank, but the oozing pus didn't abate. Emily frowned, and her hands glowed brighter.

Ralph dropped his hand over hers, curling his fingers around hers to stop her magic. "I appreciate your trying, but healing magic can't fix this. The magic that got me was red."

Char couldn't stifle this gasp. Red magic was the rarest, and there were really only two professions for which it was applicable: farming…and assassination. Red magic was growth and decay. It could be used to help a field of wheat flourish during a drought, or to help compost decompose into soil faster. And, it could be used to kill quickly, destroying a human body with brutal efficiency. The puss and poisoned skin were caused by decay, and Ralph was right that healing magic couldn't fix that.

"Then let me fix it," Karl interjected, gently pushing Emily aside. His hands glowed red and Char swallowed hard. All three kids had magic, and Karl had red magic. Just who were they? Although he'd love to know, at the moment Char was really only thankful they were here to help.

The pus vanished first, and then Ralph's skin returned to its normal color. The cut bled red for a few moments, and then that too sealed. A second later, the only evidence Ralph had ever been injured was the terrible state of his pants. Ralph stood slowly, testing his leg while shooting Karl a look that said they would be having a long talk later. All he said, though, was "Let's get out of here."

They were apparently in a basement of some kind. The door had a small window in it, but the kids had left it wide open when they arrived. Outside the door was a staircase, which led up into another hallway and a second set of stairs. They crept along, Ralph in the lead, stopping frequently to listen for anyone coming. At the top of the second stairs, Karl pointed to a closed door directly across the hall. Ralph obeyed, looking both ways in the hall before dashing across and pushing the door open. He looked around quickly and waved, so the rest of them ran for it, tumbling into the room. Ralph shut the door of what appeared to be a sitting room. Couches and a coffee table dominated the space, but the open window on the opposite wall was the most welcome sight Char had ever seen.

"Do you know if they have any guards outside?" Ralph whispered.

Karl shook his head. "This is some noble's house. The guards are all inside, because someone would notice if they had them outside. This leads to the kitchen garden, which has an unlocked back gate. We can sprint into the alley behind the house and be out of reach."

Ralph nodded, glancing out the window. "Right. Emily and Shan, you go first."

Shan helped Emily up and out of the window, gently lowering her down in a maneuver they had clearly used before. They dashed across the garden below and out the gate on the other side without any alarms being raised.

"Char, you and Karl next. I'll be right behind you."

Char nodded and slid out the window. The drop was only a few feet. Char pressed against the wall while he waited for Karl to get down, and then they sprinted together across the overgrown grass and weeds. The back of Char's neck burned the entire way; he was certain an arrow or something sharp was imminent in his back, and yet he slid to a stop outside the gate and ducked down, hidden behind the stone wall completely unharmed. Ralph dashed into view a second later, and Char was happy to see his leg was moving just fine.

"Which way?" Ralph asked Karl, who gripped Emily's hand and headed off, deeper into the warren of servant's alleys connecting the noble's residences, the rest of the group following close behind.

They traveled for a long time; the alleys went almost all the way to the part of the city where the servants lived, and Karl apparently knew exactly where to go. They eventually stopped at the end of a dark, narrow dead end, the houses on either side practically leaning on each other. A cracked wooden door at the end looked like the entrance to what, at one point, was supposed to be a root cellar shared by both houses but was empty now. Karl strained to get the cellar door open, then hopped down into the darkness. A match flared and then an oil lamp with cracked glass blazed to life. Karl reappeared at the door, holding his arms up. Emily climbed down with Karl's help, and Shan went after her. Char and Ralph followed, and Karl shut the door.

"This is—was—our hideout," Karl explained.

Char tried to keep his pity hidden. The nest of old, dirty rags was clearly the bed. Pressed against the wall, a table with a cracked leg was the only furniture. The place was dank and dark, with dirt floors and walls, but it was a palace in comparison to the room they had just escaped.

"Who else knows it's here?" Ralph asked, glancing around as well, although Char assumed he was thinking more in terms of defense than pity.

"Used to have Teddy in our group, but he was snapped up by one of the big gangs and hasn't been back in two years," Karl explained. "I don't think anyone else knows we den here."

Ralph let out a breath. "Okay, we need to get help. I need one of you to get me to the nearest guard station. Char, you have to stay hidden. If anyone comes, and I'm not with them, fight and run." He glanced around at them all. "Understand?"

"I'll show you the way," Shan said. "That way Karl can stay to fight."

Ralph looked at Karl for a long moment before letting out a breath as he apparently came to a decision. "As your commanding officer, I'm ordering you to use your magic if you get attacked. Understand?"

Karl gulped but nodded. "I'll keep Chef safe."

Ralph grinned. "You've done a great job with the rescue so far. We'd probably both be dead if you three hadn't found us, you know."

"Your kidnappers weren't as hidden as they thought, not when we know the back ways better than them. They kept having to stop to check a map," Karl added, derision coloring his voice.

Ralph shared a snicker with Karl, before sobering. "Okay. I should be back soon, although I expect the commander will want to be here too. Stay safe," Ralph finished. He climbed back out of the cellar, waited for Shan to follow, and shut the door firmly. He would be back soon with help, and until then, Char just had to breathe and believe he was safe again.

Chapter Twenty

CHAR JOINED KARL, sitting on the floor next to the lamp. Emily giggled as she burrowed into the nest of blankets, then rolled over and went straight to sleep.

"Beds are still an amazing novelty to her," Karl admitted, smiling fondly at Emily. "She was too young when our foster parents died to remember."

"Foster parents?" Char asked. He hadn't wanted to question Karl about his past before, not when it was clearly a difficult subject. Besides, Karl had always been reserved, always cognizant of the fact that he was in trouble. Even when he snuck Emily and Shan into the military compound, he had been careful and polite, and so hopeful, and Char hadn't felt right interrogating him. Perhaps Fen had, but he hadn't shared any of that with Char.

Karl slumped, sighing. "It's a quiet service nobles like to use. I have no idea if it's legal, but no one's stopped them. Any embarrassing children—bastards from affairs, children from unmarried mothers, or just general embarrassments—this service takes them all. Raises them as comfortable peasants. We're not supposed to know our origins, but we figure it out pretty quickly, especially when we learn we can't attend any of the crown schools to learn how to use our powers because we might be recognized." He paused to shake his head. "One of the big gangs figured out our foster parents had a lot more money than they should and tried to rob them. They died in the attack, and we were forced onto the streets. Now you know everything."

Karl had then attempted to pick Jensen's pocket and was sentenced to work off his crime, after which he successfully conned the royal guard into taking all three of them.

"Is Emily really your sister?" Char asked.

Karl nodded. "I'm pretty sure we had the same father but different mothers. The same servant came with money every month for us both, although I have no idea which noble our father actually is."

Char couldn't promise anything he couldn't follow through with, but he wanted to tell Karl he wouldn't have to worry any longer. Captain Zain had clearly adopted Emily, and Char wasn't about to give up Karl or Shan. He had a feeling Fen was on the same page, but he needed Fen's permission before he could offer the kids anything permanent.

For now, he simply smiled at Karl and said, "I'm certainly glad to have met you, and not just for what you did today. You're becoming very good at making bread, you know."

Karl grinned, and then his smile faded into a grimace. "I'm cheating a bit. My magic tells me whether the yeast is blooming and lets me help it grow if it's struggling."

Char blinked, surprised. He knew red magic was used to help things grow, which was why farmers were the primary—legal—users. Char had never considered things like yeast could also be manipulated that way.

"I wonder if you can take a sprouted onion that's gotten too tough to cook with and make it regress to simply being ripe?"

Karl shrugged. "Red magic isn't understood all that well, and even if I could have gone to one of the crown schools, I would have been stuffed into either farming or killing. I was considering making fake papers for Emily when she's older to get her into a school, and for Shan too, but my magic is too narrow so I've been ignoring it until now."

"Tell you what. When we get back to the military compound, we're going to set aside some onions and potatoes to let them get really over-grown and see what your magic can do. Yes, there are limitations, and yes, there are certain expectations for each type of magic, but in my experience your magic is only constrained by your imagination. Let's find out just what you can actually do."

This time Karl's smile didn't fade, and he let out a laugh. "Okay. Let's do that!"

They lapsed into silence as they waited, the long minutes passing achingly slow. Char tried not to jump at every creak and crack, but half expected the door to fly open and the dark stranger to descend on them again. He didn't know how much time had passed, but he put his inner chef's clock to good use and estimated it was at least two hours before he heard voices and the clop and jingle of horses in the alley outside.

Someone knocked on the door, followed by Ralph's far too welcome voice. "Hey, we're coming in!"

The door opened and Ralph appeared in the space. He stepped aside and Fen replaced him. Char didn't know what noise he made, only that he dashed forward, and within seconds, Fen's warm, strong arms were around him, holding him close and rocking him side to side as Char buried his face into Fen's shoulder.

At some point, Char realized Fen was whispering a repeated litany of comfort into his ear, "It's okay. I've got you. You're safe."

When Char eventually pulled away, he only went as far as arm's length, still glad to be wrapped in Fen's embrace. Fen freed one hand to gently run his thumb under Char's eyes, wiping away any evidence Char had been crying.

"Did they hurt you? Do you need a healer?" Fen asked, his eyes focused on Char, searching Char's face as if a minute change in expression could provide all the answers he wanted.

Char shook his head. "No, they only tied me up and threatened me. They got distracted and left for a bit, which is when the kids came to the rescue."

Ralph let out a heavy sigh. "Yeah, you won't believe who had come to their door. Apparently, a group of guards was assigned to every neighborhood to conduct a search of each house, and the one for that particular noble's house was out front while we were climbing out a back window. Had we used the main roads in our escape, we would have seen them and been rescued hours ago."

"I was supervising the groups searching the warehouse district," Fen explained. "Ralph and Shan found Jensen, who sent someone to find me while he led the raid on the house you escaped from. Ralph and I came straight here."

"Do you think Jensen was able to catch them?" Char asked, hopeful the dark stranger was arrested and all his terrible threats neutralized.

Unfortunately, both Ralph and Fen shook their heads. "Too much time went by after you all escaped," Fen explained. "They probably had more than enough time to find you gone and then run. Although, if we're lucky, they won't have had enough time to destroy all the evidence, so we'll hopefully get something out of the raid. I should have a report from Jensen soon."

The light from inside the cellar went out and Char turned to see Karl carefully closing the door, Emily yawning and rubbing her eyes at his side. A glance upward revealed the sun had set at some point, and the alley was being brightly lit by mage lights. They started walking down the alley, heading to the main road. Char's arm brushed against Fen's as they went, sending warmth and comfort with every touch.

Char didn't know what made him look up again, nor how he noticed the dark shape partially obscured behind the shine of the bright lights, but when the shadow tensed and leaped, Char shouted and shoved, sending Fen sprawling out of the way of the long knife that slashed the air where he had just been standing.

The dark stranger straightened from where they had landed and then lunged, the knife aiming for Char, who was able to deflect it, his hands and arms glowing bright blue. The knife's edge suddenly took on a red sheen—assassin's magic. This time when the stranger lunged, the knife slid right through Char's magic, scoring a deep line across the back of his arm in a flare of pain that had Char yelping, his tears already streaming.

"Char!" Fen yelled. He slid between Char and the stranger, slashing with a sword glowing brilliant gold. The red knife slid aside, parried easily as the royal magic overpowered the assassin's.

They were surrounded, Char realized. Fen, Ralph, and the half-dozen guards they had brought along were fighting at least fifteen assailants. The narrow alley hampered everyone. Swords were too long to swing properly, and they kept bumping into each other. Even the assailants appeared to regret their choice of ambush location since all fifteen couldn't attack at once. Only the stranger with their long knife, rather than a sword, and the two kids, who also only had knives, weren't having trouble. Karl and Emily darted between the fighters, slashing and stabbing as they went, dropping assailants with far more ease than the seasoned guards.

Char stood in the middle of it all, clutching at his arm and feeling helpless, trying to stifle the tears still streaming down his cheeks. He was a chef, not a fighter, but there had to be something he could do to help. Someone had left a knife on the ground. Char scooped it up with the hand of his uninjured arm and glanced around, hoping to find some way to help.

Everywhere he looked was absolute mayhem. Fen was fighting the stranger, his gold-glowing sword clashing against the red-glowing long knife. The longer reach of the sword was hampered by the tight confines of the alley, but Fen was clearly the more skilled of the two so it wasn't hampering him much. Ralph took on two fighters, and as Fen watched, he skewered the one on the left, kicked her off his sword, and turned to engage the one on his right. Karl darted between the fighters, slashing and jabbing with a bloodied knife in each hand. He got one fighter in the side, the man immediately collapsing and letting the royal guard turn to another opponent. Emily was... Char cast around, trying to figure out where she was, and finally caught sight of her as a group of fighters moved past Char and deeper into the alley. She was creeping up behind one of the assailants, who had cornered a guard against a trash bin. Slow and stealthy, like a cat. Except, behind her was another attacker, grinning. He swung his blade as Char dived forward, and the metal slid harmlessly off Char's blue-glowing arm.

A scream from behind him said Emily had found her mark, but Char couldn't turn to look. All his attention was focused on the man in front of him who slashed and stabbed at Char, snarling when his short sword bounced harmlessly away from Char's exposed flesh. The last slash sent the man's arm careening wide as the impact with Char's magic sent the sword skittering away. Char saw the opening and took it, lunging forward.

Stabbing a human wasn't all that different from stabbing a side of beef. An initial puncture through the skin, then resistance that tried to punch the knife back at Char—the hilt sliding in his hand until he tightened his grip—and then smooth gliding as the knife reached the softer bits inside. However, dead animals didn't let out a terrible scream, nor did hot blood start gushing and flowing over Char's hand, making his already tenuous grip too slick to hold onto as the man jerked back. The man stumbled back another step, Char's knife sticking out the right side of his stomach, and gaped, his mouth open like a fish out of water.

And then, suddenly, the alley was full of guards. Zain strode into view, and Char let out a heavy sigh of relief. One of the attackers lunged for her, and Zain casually slapped him aside, her gauntlet slicing his face open, and her strength sending him slamming against the alley wall. He lay where he fell.

"I leave you alone for five minutes!" she snarled.

Emily popped up at Zain's side, the baby chick returning to her mother, as Zain walked through the fighting as if she were strolling through a meadow on her way to a picnic. She glanced at Char, covered in blood, most of which wasn't his own, and lifted an eyebrow, but she quickly focused on Fen.

"What are you doing, boy?" she snapped, her voice booming through the alley. "Stop prolonging the fight!"

Fen let out a long sigh and rolled his shoulders as if they were tight. "Do you surrender?" Fen asked.

The stranger didn't reply, charging forward as his knife traced a pattern in the air. Fen stepped into it and leaned to the side so the knife passed harmlessly to his left. Char didn't see him move, but the golden sword was suddenly sticking out the other side of the stranger. More blood flowed, and the body collapsed, boneless, as it slid off the sword to flop on the ground.

"Bring one of those lights over!" Zain commanded as she strode over to Fen, who was bending down. He freed his sword first, then used the tip to drag the dark hood away from the stranger's face. Sightless gold-brown eyes stared out of a face frozen in a snarl. Familiar, gold-brown eyes. Char turned just in time to see Karl step forward, the same colored eyes gazing down at the dead man.

"Was he my father?" Karl asked, his voice tight with what sounded like anger.

"If I had to guess," Fen replied after a moment of thought, "I would say this is probably your uncle. Baron Whistfield is more likely to be your father, since he would have the motivation to hide bastard children. His wife is the younger daughter of an earl who would be very displeased—in terms of continuing to fund Whistfield's political and social calendar—to find out he's cheating on her. If I remember correctly, though, this is Lord

Oliver."

"Oliver is his older brother's stooge," Zain cut in. "I'm going to take a contingent to go and have a chat with dear Baron Whistfield if you think you can stay out of trouble for long enough, that is," she added to Fen. Fen quirked an eyebrow at her, and she sighed. "With your permission, Commander."

"Permission granted."

She saluted and trotted off, about half her guards going with her. Fen turned to Ralph next.

"I want the prisoners interrogated and the bodies searched. And we should make sure to prepare Lord Oliver's body for his brother's viewing."

Ralph saluted and started calling out orders, striding off down the alley toward the dead end where a group of surviving attackers was being searched for weapons. Fen turned to Char next, frowning heavily as he took in the blood and dirt covering Char from head to foot.

"The red magic got you, right?" Karl asked as he hurried to Char's side. His hand glowed red briefly as he held it over Char's injured arm. The pain vanished immediately, fading away as if he had never been injured, and Char let out a relieved sigh.

"I think all of us need to go home, take a bath, and get some sleep," Fen said. Apparently, Ralph had filled him in about the kids' magic, because he didn't miss a beat due to surprise. He finally led the way out of the alley and into the street. Horses had scattered everywhere, but Fen whistled, and the one he usually rode trotted over. Fen mounted and pulled Char up to sit behind him. A second guard came over with another horse. He hoisted Emily up into the saddle, climbed up behind her, and then yanked Karl up to sit pillion behind him.

Char fell asleep during the ride, Fen's hand over the arms Char had wrapped around his waist pretty much the only thing that kept him in the saddle. He was groggy when they dismounted but followed where Fen led, which was eventually to a large bathing room with both an overhead shower and a sunken tub.

Char stepped into the hot water flowing from the shower spigot, letting it run over his body. Blood dripped off him, turning the tile floor first red and then pink, before the water ran clear again. Char was shaking, he realized, as he stepped aside to let Fen reach the water and to get some soap. Fen stood under the water for only a brief couple of seconds to let the outer layer of blood and dirt wash off before gently grabbing Char and pulling him into his arms.

"It's okay. We're all okay," Fen whispered into Char's hair, holding him tight as those simple words released a torrent inside Char. Tears flowed, dripping down his cheeks to be washed away by the water exactly the same as the blood had done.

"I killed a man," Char said, his voice broken and choked. "I felt the knife go into him, and then all that blood, and he was dead."

"I saw what you did; you saved Emily's life," Fen cut in. "You stopped a man who would have enjoyed killing a child. And that's after saving my life." He paused, one hand stroking down Char's back. "It's good you feel guilty. That means your soul is still intact. But you shouldn't let that guilt define you because what you did was for the right reasons. No one would ever fault you for that, so don't fault yourself."

Char listened to Fen's soft, gently cajoling voice and finally his tears slowed. He turned his face up into the spray, washing away the tightness on his face, wishing the water was enough to also wash away the aching hole he felt inside. Yet, Fen's words helped soothe that too. Char doubted it would ever completely go away, but by the time Fen released him and let Char resume locating soap, he no longer felt as if he ought to be the one arrested in that alley. When they tumbled into the bed together in the next room, Char immediately fell back to sleep, curled up with Fen's strength surrounding him, and didn't wake until someone knocked on the door the next morning.

Chapter Twenty-One

"WHERE ARE WE?" Char asked. He sat up in bed, the covers pooled in his lap, as he stared around the room. He hadn't been coherent enough last night to notice, plus it had been dark, but the place was very, very nice. The four-poster bed they had slept in was massive, with a deep, extremely comfortable mattress and velvet curtains they hadn't bothered to close. The walls had cloth wallpaper in wide stripes of blue and cream and along the walls the furniture was all beautifully carved dark-stained wood.

Fen let out a low groan as he rolled over, and he buried his nose into Char's side and threw one arm around Char's waist.

"My bedroom," Fen explained, the words slightly muffled but clear enough to send a jolt of adrenaline through Char's body.

"In the palace?" he squeaked out.

Fen chuckled and squeezed Char in a gentle hug. "If just being in my room in the palace is scary, wait until you see who we're about to have breakfast with."

Char let out a whimper. "Can't I just go back to the military compound? I should be there anyway, making breakfast for your troops." This was the first time in Char's memory that he had slept right through his normal waking hour. He felt rested, and after yesterday that was a surprisingly good feeling, but at the same time he felt antsy as if he was supposed to be somewhere else and doing something else.

"They'll survive another morning without you," Fen said. He sighed and finally sat up. "Besides. If I let you run off now when I know how much my mother has been dying to meet you, she'll hunt you down. It'll be easier today since we can distract her with reports of everything that happened last night, anyway. So, let's get dressed and get it over with, and maybe you'll be back in your kitchen with enough time to throw something together for dinner."

Char bit his lip, worried, but he nodded. If he wanted to continue his relationship with Fen, he would need to meet Fen's parents eventually. And Fen was right; with everything that had happened yesterday as a distraction, meeting them today would be easier.

Fen found him clean clothing. Once they were both dressed, Fen led the way out of the bedroom, through a grand sitting room Char had taken no notice of the previous evening, and out into a lushly appointed hallway. They didn't go too far—Char's steps sinking into the luxurious carpet as they walked only about a minute—stopping in front of another door in the same hall. Fen held the door open for Char, who walked into a small dining room where almost every seat at the table was already taken.

"Oh? Did my dear baby brother sleep well last night, while the rest of us were busy cleaning up his mess?" one of the people sitting at the table jeered. He appeared to be in his midtwenties and looked similar to Fen, so Char thought this was one of Fen's brothers. There were two younger men and one older—the king, and Char was mentally hyperventilating about being in the same room as the king—plus two women and a handful of children.

"Shut it, Braxton," Fen replied, heading to one of the two empty seats around the table. He pulled one out and held it for Char to sit before taking his own. "Fill me in."

"While you were getting your beauty rest, some of us spent the night going through Baron Whistfield's estate," Braxton paused to take a pointed gulp of his black tea before continuing. "The man was a slob and didn't know the first thing about organization, but what we did find had Namin stamped all over it."

"You'll be glad to know he was apprehended attempting to flee the city and has been singing like a songbird ever since," the other brother—who had to be Crown Prince Ayer—said.

"What that means, since my sons appear to think it's a game to string you along like this," the queen cut in, speaking directly to Char, "is the threat against you has been neutralized. I am certain the enemy will continue to place spies and potential assassins in the royal guard, but the plan to coerce Fen's new chef into participating in Namin's plot was purely Whistfield's idea. Now that the plot has failed so spectacularly, they will be forced to find a new target."

Char swallowed down his nerves. He glanced at Fen, who smiled, and then looked back at the queen. "Thank you, Your Majesty. Um, that's good to know they won't be targeting me because I'm Fen's chef. But what about if I'm…" He glanced at Fen again as his words trailed off.

Queen Trina laughed. "Oh, they most definitely won't target you now you're in a relationship with Fen. You've proven your loyalty to him quite admirably, to the point you helped take down a baron. They won't waste time trying to flip you again."

What she wasn't saying was Char was a bigger target for assassination than before, that hurting him would in turn hurt Fen, but that was something Char already knew. Fen's role as prince and commander always meant anyone he fell in love with would have to face that threat, something Char had completely understood before he walked up that staircase those few short weeks ago. With Baron Whistfield neutralized, Char hoped even that threat was reduced.

Before he could think of how to respond, someone knocked on the door and then Zain let herself into the room. She bowed quickly and then went over to Ayer and Braxton, handing them each large sheaves of paper.

"Completed reports from last night," she explained, bowing again. "We've rounded up the last of the fighters Whistfield brought in, all two hundred. I'll have the reports of their interviews this afternoon."

"Thank you, Captain," Ayer said, nodding in reply. "Give your report to your commander and then take a few hours for yourself to rest."

"Your Majesties," she said with yet another bow, before turning and making her way over to where Fen and Char were sitting.

"I checked up on the things you asked me," she said to Fen after nodding hello to them both. "The guard taking those convenient nighttime breaks was being bribed by three different people to be away from the gate at that time. He didn't know who snuck in or out, just that he was making a lot of money. We've narrowed one of the payments to Whistfield, but the other two are going to take a bit more time to figure out."

"Good work," Fen replied. "Have Captain Wong and Jensen work with Commander Tenisen on the rest of that case. You're doing enough cleaning up after Whistfield. What about the rest?"

Zain nodded. "Sherri is still in the palace healers' wing, but the healers believe she should be safe to move to the military compound's wing later this week. All indications are she'll make a full recovery." Char let out a relieved breath at those words. He had been wondering where Sherri was after that terrible battle but hadn't found a chance to ask. Hearing she was going to be okay was amazing. "All three kids were returned to the compound safely last night," Zain continued. "I gave them the day off from school so they have today to recuperate. That said, I'm going to arrange for them to have regular training with the troops after school. They did well in the fighting, but with a little training I think they could really become something. Er, with your permission, of course," she tacked on awkwardly, no doubt remembering the last time she had blithely accepted one of the kids without first consulting with Fen.

Fen chuckled. "Permission granted, although if the two boys are going to be helping Char in the kitchen too, you can't keep them at drill all afternoon."

"Understood. I have a feeling Karl and Shan would object if I kept them out of the kitchen anyway." She chuckled. "The girl Emily will be commander someday. I swear it."

"That could very well be true," Fen replied, grinning. "Thank you for checking up on them. Anything else to report?"

Zain smirked and looked at Char. "Only that I was asked to tell Chef his donkey was recovered from the city. Someone located the shopping list and what appears to be a thousand canning jars are taking up half the kitchen. Someone asked if you would be canning figs, since they're in season right now."

It was Char's turn to smile. "I'm glad Wise One made it home safe too. My fruit and vegetable supplier sends me whatever is in season, so if I get some figs I'll definitely preserve them. Please tell Jensen to authorize reimbursement to whomever purchased my jars," Char added. He really wanted to be back in his kitchen now, boiling fruits for jams and vinegar for pickling. He had a lot still to put away in preparation for winter.

Fen let out a soft chuckle and reached out to grip Char's hand, reminding Char where he was and why he couldn't run off just yet.

"Now, as my brother said, take some time to rest and recuperate," Fen added to Zain. "Dismissed."

Zain saluted before turning and walking to the door, dodging servants pushing carts full of cloche-covered trays into the room as she left. One servant deposited a plate in front of Char, and a second filled his teacup, and when Char looked up again it was to see Fen's entire family looking at him. Char gulped and looked down again.

The pancakes looked reasonably fluffy, so they hadn't been overmixed. The fresh fruit in a bowl to the side had evenly cut melon squares, the color distribution was pleasing to the eye, and there was a good balance between tart citrus versus sweet berry. Two small pitchers filled the rest of the plate. The first proved to be syrup and the second a mixed berry compote that, at a glance, had Char's alarm bells ringing. He took a spoon and dipped it into the compote, carefully licking the liquid off the back of the spoon before it could drip on the tablecloth. He grimaced, suspicions confirmed. Far too much lemon and slightly undercooked, so the natural pectin from the fruit hadn't had time to properly thicken. A glance around the table identified the sugar bowl. Char might not be able to fix the cooking time, but a quarter teaspoon of sugar would help with the sourness.

He scooped the right amount of sugar into his pitcher, grabbed the one from Fen's plate and added sugar there too. He stirred both and tasted again, then let out a sigh. The texture was all wrong, but at least the compote would be palatable on the tongue now.

Char looked up when he realized multiple people were laughing. Queen Trina had her mouth hidden behind one hand, but Prince Ayer and Prince Braxton weren't bothering to hide their mirth. Char's cheeks heated, and he ducked his head, looking down at his lap rather than the food.

"Please don't be embarrassed," Queen Trina said, her tone gentle and, while still full of laughter, was not chiding. "It's only, Fen described you to us with perfect accuracy. Here we are, ready to interrogate you as any good family must of their child's significant other, and then the food arrived, and all your fear vanished. You were more incensed by the poor showing from our kitchen than worried about us. It is quite adorable, you know."

"Um," Char mumbled, wishing he could think of something articulate to say.

"Adding a bit of sugar will make this fruit thing edible?" Prince Braxton asked, swirling the pitcher so the much too loose liquid splashed along the edges.

Food Char could talk about without worry, and his response fell out before he thought about what to say. "Compote. And, um, a quarter teaspoon of sugar will add enough sweetness to balance the sour lemon. But I can't do anything about the texture," Char added, growling slightly over the last part.

"How would you fix that?" Shairon asked while Braxton stole the sugar bowl from her.

"Cook it longer. A good compote only takes maybe ten minutes to make. I would guess they only spent five on this one."

"Has cooking always been your main interest?" Queen Trina asked. Once everyone had added sugar to their compote, they began eating.

Char nodded. "It's a tradition in the Musen family. I've been helping in the kitchen since before I could walk."

They asked him more generalized questions about his family and his hobbies, which Char answered while he ate the passable food. Midway through, Fen's hand slipped into Char's, their fingers tangling together. They shared a brief smile, and Char realized any remaining worry about meeting Fen's family had faded away sometime while they were talking.

Their duties might keep them apart sometimes, but the love Char felt for Fen and the love Char saw gleaming out of Fen's smile, said whatever the future might bring they would still be happy together.

Interlude

BRAXTON WALKED DOWN the last of the steps into the dungeons, stepping onto stone-flagged floors that were cheap but easy to mop. Only political prisoners ended up in the palace dungeons; the prison complex for everyone else was about five miles north of the city, heavily fortified with specialty guards. Braxton didn't like going there, so it was nice Prince Clament was one of their pampered guests here in the palace. Braxton visited every couple days to ask one simple question.

He walked down the hall, which had barred doors for six cells, three on either side, and stopped outside the last door on the right, peering through the bars at the lone person lying on the bed inside. Prince Clament had the blond hair and blue eyes of his entire family, the royal family of Namin. Normally, those brilliant blue eyes were glaring at the door, fierce and powerful and wonderfully defiant even with hair disheveled from months in a cell. This time, Clament was curled into a ball, huddled underneath the thin blanket.

"Are you ready to talk?" Braxton asked, his usual question feeling flat today.

Clament didn't answer, and Braxton thought he might be shivering.

Braxton turned to one of the guards stationed in this wing. "Summon the healer," he ordered. The man dashed off, and Braxton turned to a second one. "Open this door."

The second man produced a key ring and fitted the key into the lock, which groaned as the lock was turned. The door hinges let out a screech as the guard yanked it open. And Clament didn't twitch.

Braxton hurried inside, his two personal guards following closely, and paused at Clament's side. He was definitely shivering, his nose curled up to his knees, and clutching at the blanket in clenched fists. Braxton slowly reached out, tentatively resting his palm against Clament's forehead, then yanked his hand back with a hiss. Clament's skin was boiling.

"Why the hell am I back here so soon?" someone whined from the hallway. "I just put this bastard back together last night! Can't you wait a few days before ripping him to pieces?"

Braxton sucked in a sharp breath at the healer's words, clenching his own hands into fists to keep from lashing out. There was only one reason the healer would be familiar with this particular prisoner, a reason for which his words also implied. Braxton straightened and turned to face the door, catching both prison guards and the healer in his harsh, angry glare.

"Who signed the writ approving torturing this man?" Braxton asked, his voice eerily calm, considering the fury churning inside, absolutely ready to explode like a volcano. "Answer me!" he roared.

"You wanted him to talk," the guard who had fetched the healer began, his voice a whine that had Braxton clenching his teeth and taking in slow breaths through his nose to keep from screaming again.

"The law is clear," he said, trying to sound reasonable and logical when all he really wanted to do was grab the guard and shake him until the stupid fell out. "Torture of political prisoners requires a royal writ, signed by the king or crown prince, and sealed by whichever one didn't sign. Tell me where you got a writ to touch this man?" Braxton prowled closer, and his two personal guards spread out to encircle the three men.

"You want answers, this is how you get them," the guard continued, still whining but sounding even more desperate as he glanced around the small space.

"Hands in the air. You're under arrest. All of you," Braxton added pointedly to the healer, who had opened his mouth to protest.

Slowly, all three obeyed, although the loudmouthed guard and healer both looked like they wanted to argue. One of Braxton's guards—Mark—moved forward to disarm the two guards. He checked the healer, but he wasn't carrying anything. The other of Braxton's guards—Sapson—drew his sword and stood ready to intervene if needed. Braxton watched, arms crossed and scowling, seething inside.

How dare these mere guards presume to know what Braxton wanted! How dare they touch Clament! All of his fire, his fierce beauty, shuttered and hidden behind a thin blanket and high fever. And there was no telling what mental issues Clament now bore, since torture was more effective at breaking a man than getting actual answers.

"Luckily we're already in a prison," Braxton said, bending down to retrieve one of the sets of keys on the ground next to the pile of weapons. He passed the keys to Mark. "Mark, put them each in their own cell.

Quickly. I need to get Prince Clament to the healers' wing."

Mark took the keys and dragged the three prisoners away, Sapson following, sword still at the ready. Braxton left them to it, turning to Clament. He gently slid his arms underneath the curled body, feeling the shivering rattling through his own bones, and picked Clament up. Clament's golden head rested against Braxton's shoulder, his puffing, panting breaths blowing against Braxton's neck. He started walking out of the prison, heading for the secret passages that would keep Clament's presence and illness secret from gossipmongers and spies alike. Mark and Sapson caught up quickly, following as Braxton led the way through the passages to the healers' wing, hoping he wasn't too late to save Clament's life.

Epilogue

CHAR WAS BUSY scraping the meat out of pie pumpkins, the flesh still steaming as they were fresh from baking in the oven, when a pair of arms wrapped around him from behind.

"If you make me drop a pumpkin..." Char growled, trailing off threateningly. His pumpkin-coated hands glowed faintly blue as his magic protected him from the heat, and he held them up and away from the arms hugging Char into a warm and very familiar chest.

"It's the Frost Festival!" Fen exclaimed. "You're supposed to have fun!"

"I am having fun," Char growled. "I'm baking. I promised to deliver a thousand hand pies to the festival grounds in time for the dance tonight!"

"How much longer will it take? I want to steal you away to go look through the stalls. And there're a lot of games set up on the back lawn too."

Char sighed. A glance over at Karl said the dough was almost done.

Karl was already rolling it out, his circle cutter ready to start making the correct shapes. Shan was bagging all the leftover seeds, which Char would clean and roast for a festive snack to offer back at the barracks. All that was left was the filling of pumpkin, evaporated milk, eggs, and spices, which he had just been yanked away from.

"Another hour, if you stop distracting me. Can you wait that long?"

Fen let out a huff but started laughing a second later. He stepped back, finally releasing Char, and his smile was electric.

"How about I help out instead? Another set of hands and you might be done sooner." Fen went over to one of the sinks located in the corner of the massive cooking tent, set up specifically for the festival, to wash his hands. The space was full of cooks and chefs from all around the country, all of whom had been contracted to serve at least one dish sometime during the festival. Even Terrance was actually cooking something on the other side of the tent. The palace kitchens were far too small to fit everyone, so the temporary tent was used.

Char returned to scooping cooked pumpkin. The sooner he got it out of the shells, the faster it would cool to the point he could safely add eggs without scrambling them.

Fen went to help Karl with the dough, leaving Char to focus on getting his spice mixture correct and getting the pumpkin ready to fill the pie shells. Normal pumpkin pie was loose until it was baked; Char would have preferred to use miniature tart shells rather than hand pies for pumpkin, but there weren't enough tart tins. Instead he had altered the ratios of ingredients to make a thicker filling without compromising on taste. Once the filling was ready, Char showed Shan how much to place in the center of each dough circle, then showed Karl and Fen how to fold and crimp the edges. Once the edges were secure, Char gave the outside a quick egg wash, and then the pies went into the oven. Even with Fen's help, they still took the full hour, but finally the last of the pies were out of the oven and cooling on a rack.

Char gave his instructions to one of the kitchen servants. There was an entire cadre of servants assigned to the kitchen tent solely responsible for boxing and delivering the completed food. Once that was done, he turned to the kids.

"Here's some money. Buy some dinner for yourselves, and if you see something at the shops you'd like, go ahead and buy it." Char held out more than enough money for Karl and Shan to enjoy themselves at the festival. But, when Karl gripped the money, Char didn't let go. "Stay out of trouble," he added pointedly, giving them his best suspicious, parental eyeing.

"We'll be good. Promise, Chef," Karl replied.

Char smiled and let go. "I'll hold you to that."

Karl split the money in half, sharing it with Shan. "We're gonna go find Emily," Karl said, waving as they ran off. "I think she's at the weapons expo with Zain."

They vanished into the crowd, and Char turned toward Fen, who held out a hand for Char to take.

Walking together, hand in hand, was a rare pleasure. Char luxuriated in the uninterrupted time to just be a couple. No soldiers running up with tasks for Fen to complete. No more meals to prep for the rest of the day. They were both free of all responsibilities until tomorrow morning, which was glorious. They left the palace grounds and walked to the largest park where shopkeepers had set up tents, singers and actors had set up stages, and what appeared to be the entire city had descended. Many neighborhoods had their own, smaller festival areas, and bars and restaurants throughout the city were offering specials for the holiday, but this was the best and most exciting place to be.

Outside the kitchen tent, the air was brisk with midwinter chill, although serious snow wouldn't begin falling until next month. That and the crush of people gave Char an excuse to cuddle close to Fen. They went through the food area first, tasting the samples of cheeses and spreads on offer and checking out the stalls selling pots and pans. Char obtained a number of business cards for places to contact after the festival had ended, including a company offering a nonstick coating on metal saucepans that the company claimed allowed for reduced oil or butter in the cooking process to allow for healthier meals. They shared a massive funnel cake covered in powdered sugar, which ended up being lunch since it was so big. Next, Char happily followed Fen over to where weapons merchants had set up their stalls, and they spent a while perusing swords, knives, and armor.

All in all, it was a lovely afternoon. Only when the sun began to dip, the adjacent buildings casting long shadows over the park, did they return to the palace. Char was getting used to being in Fen's room, at least. He spent a couple nights a month there with Fen. However, he still felt odd wandering through the rest of the palace. He was allowed full access to pretty much the entire building, but usually stayed with Fen or in Fen's room. Tonight, though, he was trying to put aside that awkward feeling.

"Are you sure I should be wearing this?" Char asked, plucking at the leg of the vermillion suit Fen had him put on. The jacket was embroidered in a design of feathers in more reds, oranges, and yellows, and Char missed his boring and utilitarian brown pants and white shirt. Fen shrugged into a cobalt blue jacket embroidered with the same feathers, only in blues and purples, before turning to survey Char. His smile was slow and full of heat, a definite promise for later that had Char half wishing they could skip the dance entirely.

"We can't go to a masque without a costume. We are two stages of the lifespan of the mythical phoenix," he added as he reached back into the box their outfits had come out of and retrieved two masks. They were identical aside from the color: pointed beaks and dyed feathers to look like a bird's face. Fen handed Char the blue one, rather than the red. Mentally shrugging, Char slipped it on, wondering whether Fen knew his need to use the mask to mark Char as his was so damned adorable.

"Besides," Fen continued, grinning cheekily. "You know you want to go to the dance to see how your pumpkin things turned out."

Char stuck his tongue out at Fen, even though Fen was right about the hand pies. However, what Char really wanted he already had. Fen slid an arm over Char's shoulder, pulling him into a hug. Char cuddled close.

"I am glad I decided not to kill you," Fen murmured into Char's hair, his nose nuzzling along Char's ear.

Char pushed his mask up out of the way and pressed his lips firmly to Fen's. "I'm glad too."

Recipes

For my readers who found Char's brownies, mac 'n cheese, and chicken pot pie too delicious to resist. I asked my editor to pick the recipes that made her hungriest while editing, and these three topped her list. I hope you enjoy making them as much as Char does.

Double Chocolate Brownies

INGREDIENTS

¾ c. flour

¼ tsp baking soda

¼ tsp. salt

1/3 c. butter

2 large eggs

¾ c. granulated sugar

2 T. water

12 oz. chocolate chips

1 tsp. vanilla extract

½ c. chopped nuts (peanuts, walnuts, pecans, or whichever you prefer)

DIRECTIONS
1. Preheat oven to 350° (325° for dark pans).

2. Grease 9x9-inch pan.

3. In a small bowl, combine flour, baking soda, and salt.

4. In a small saucepan combine butter, sugar, and water. Bring to just a boil, then remove from heat. Add 1 Cup/6 Oz chocolate chips and vanilla. Stir until chips melt and mixture is smooth.

5. Transfer chocolate mixture to large mixing bowl and cool. Add eggs one at a time, beating well after each addition.

6. Gradually blend in flour mixture.

7. Stir in remaining chips and nuts.

8. Bake for at least 30 minutes, until a tester comes out clean.

NOTES AND VARIATIONS:
This can be made without nuts, but it will result in a softer texture.

Mac and Cheese

INGREDIENTS

4 T. butter

½ c. yellow onion, finely chopped

4 T. flour

4 c. milk

1 tsp. salt (amount is approximate)

1 tsp. dry mustard

½ tsp. ground black pepper

16 oz. package elbow macaroni

4 c. shredded sharp cheddar cheese

16 oz. pkg. American cheese, cut into strips

1 pkg. fried onions (6oz)

DIRECTIONS

1. Preheat oven to 350°.

2. Cook macaroni according to package directions.

3. Melt butter in large saucepan over medium heat.

4. Sauté onion in butter for about two minutes (until onions become clear). Stir in flour and cook 1 minute, stirring constantly.

5. Stir in milk, salt, mustard, and pepper. Cook, stirring frequently, until mixture boils and thickens.

6. Add cheddar and American cheeses to milk mixture. Stir until cheese melts.

7. Combine macaroni with cheese mixture. Mix well. Put in 3-quart baking dish.

8. Cover mixture in the entire package of fried onions.

9. Bake uncovered for 30 minutes, or until hot and bubbly. Let cool 10 minutes before serving.

NOTES AND VARIATIONS

Panko crumbs lightly sautéed in butter can be substituted for the package of fried onions.

Shredded Monterey Jack cheese can be added with other cheeses for a creamier cheese mixture.

Chicken Pot Pie

INGREDIENTS

2 of 9-inch deep-dish frozen pie crusts, thawed

1/3 c. butter or margarine

1/3 c. chopped onion

1/3 (heaping) c. all-purpose flour

½ tsp salt

¼ tsp pepper

garlic powder to taste

onion powder to taste

powdered sage to taste

4 oz. can stems and pieces mushrooms, drained

1 can (10 – 14 oz.) chicken broth

½ c. milk

2-3 boneless, skinless chicken breasts

1 c. frozen mixed vegetables, thawed

2 small white potatoes

DIRECTIONS

1. Chicken:

a. Put 1/4 to 1/3 of the can of chicken broth in a deep-sided sauté pan. (The broth should only be deep enough to cover half the chicken.) Add half the needed garlic powder, onion powder, sage, and cracked black pepper.

b. Clean chicken and place in pan; coat visible top side of chicken with the other half of above spices.

c. Cook on medium-low, flipping halfway through.

d. Once chicken is just cooked, remove from broth, dice or shred, and set aside.

2. Potatoes:

a. Simultaneous to cooking the chicken, wash and cube potatoes.

b. Place in small saucepan with enough water to completely cover the top of the potatoes.

c. Add a dash of salt.

d. Boil until potatoes are soft enough for a fork to easily go through.

e. Drain and set aside.

3. Pot Pie:

a. Heat oven to 425°

b. In 2-quart saucepan, melt butter over medium heat.

c. Add onion and cook for 2 minutes, stirring frequently until tender.

d. Stir in flour, salt, and pepper until well blended.

e. Gradually stir in remaining broth and milk, cooking and stirring until bubbly and thickened.

f. Stir in chicken, mixed vegetables, mushrooms, and potatoes.

g. Remove from heat and spoon into one pie crust.

h. Top with second crust; seal edge by pressing with a fork.

i. Cut slits in several places in top crust.

j. Bake 25 to 30 minutes until crust is golden brown. Any longer will require covering the edges with strips of foil to prevent excessive browning.

Let stand 5 minutes before serving.

About the Author

When Mell Eight was in high school, she discovered dragons. Beautiful, wondrous creatures that took her on epic adventures both to faraway lands and on journeys of the heart. Mell wanted to create dragons of her own, so she put pen to paper. Mell Eight is now known for her own soaring dragons, as well as for other wonderful characters dancing across the pages of her books. While she mostly writes paranormal or fantasy stories, she has been seen exploring the real world once or twice.

Facebook

www.facebook.com/MellEightFiction

Twitter

www.x.com/MellEight

Website

www.melleightfiction.weebly.com

Other NineStar books by this author

Witch's Circle Series

Coven

Hunter

Witch

Ge-Mi Series

Ge-Mi, Part One

Ge-Mi, Part Two

Oracle Series

The Oracle's Flame

The Oracle's Hatchling

The Oracle's Golem

The Oracle's Sprite

The Oracle's Prophecy

The Oracle's Current

Supernatural Consultant Series

Dragon Consultant

Dragon Deception

Dragon Dilemma

Dragon Detective

Dragon Soldier

Dragon Adventures

Dragon Lesson

Out of Underhill Series

Kelpie Blue

If a Butterfly Don't Fly

Magnified Series

Magnified

Justified

Dragon's Hoard Series

Finding the Wolf

Breaking the Shackles

Stealing the Dragon

Melting the Ice Witch

Road to… Series

Road to Revenge

Road to Home

Wizard Wars Series

Ground of Insurrection

Ground of Resurrection

Standalone Books

Elemental Ride

A Little Fairy Dust

Wounded Alpha

The Coup and the Prince

Space Stars

Water's Price

Twin Elements

Soul Bond

Gifting a Dragon's Heart

www.ninestarpress.com

www.facebook.com/ninestarpress

www.facebook.com/groups/NineStarNiche

www.twitter.com/ninestarpress

www.instagram.com/ninestarpress

bsky.app/profile/ninestarpress.bsky.social

www.threads.net/@ninestarpress